SOMETHING LIKE LOVE

CHICAGO GRIZZLIES

PIPER RAYNE

This book is a work of fiction. Names, characters, places and incidents either are products of the author's imagination or are used fictitiously. Any resemblance to actual events or locales or persons, living or dead, is entirely coincidental.

© 2024 by Piper Rayne®

Piper Rayne® registered in U.S. Patent and Trademark Office.

All rights reserved, including the right to reproduce this book or portions thereof in any form whatsoever.

Cover Design: By Hang Le

1st Line Editor: Joy Editing

2nd Line Editor: My Brother's Editor

Proofreader: My Brother's Editor

ABOUT SOMETHING LIKE LOVE

I want to.

I can't.

I've been friends with Cooper Rice from the moment we met. He was just as famous a decade ago on our college campus as he is now being the star quarterback for the Chicago Grizzlies.

But he's not only talented on the field, he's also the gorgeous football star women fawn over, posing in underwear and razor ads.

Here's a secret those women don't know—Cooper Rice isn't a playboy. He's the kind of man who wants to settle down with a family. He's content ordering pizza and massaging my feet after my long shift as an emergency room doctor. He listens to me as if he's as invested as I am in my patients. He has never let me down.

This is exactly why I refuse to live without Cooper in my life. Eight years ago, I made him promise me that we'd never cross that line. And just like I knew Cooper would, he's held to that promise.

Despite our best efforts, our relationship is evolving, shifting into new territory and I find myself unsure if I want Cooper to keep that promise. Ignoring the obvious could tear us apart, but so could giving in, meaning there's a chance I'll lose Cooper forever no matter what decision I make.

SOMETHING LIKE *Love*

CHAPTER 1

COOPER

I'm not usually a guy who gets really nervous before a game. But sitting in the locker room, about to put my pads on, I have to close my eyes to get my bearings. Sweat beads along my hairline, and nausea grows in my stomach. All the commentators' remarks and predictions for this season cycle through my brain.

I've won back-to-back championships, and that's an amazing feat. Not many players before me have done it, but if I win this year, it would be my third, which is unheard of, never been done before. Everyone is watching us, especially me as the quarterback and team captain, to see if I can make it happen.

"Rice!" Coach Stone calls from his office.

Damon and Miles look in my direction. They know that, yeah, there's pressure on them to win this year, but most of the responsibility rests in the quarterback's hands. I clench and unclench my hands, staring down at them.

As I stand at the threshold of Coach's office, I say, "Hey, Coach."

"Come in." He waves me in and circles his finger for me to shut the door.

I've grown used to him since I was traded here, and I've held my spot for all these years. I don't sit because there isn't a lot of time before we need to be on the field.

"Listen, I know you're feeling the pressure. Anyone would. There've been players before you who felt it and failed to accomplish their goals. So, I just wanted to give you a piece of advice before you go out there today. Everyone is looking at us. But I don't have to tell you that because you're my most dedicated player. Never had distractions like the others." He shakes his head, and I'm pretty sure he's talking about Damon—who was in the midst of having a baby with a one-night stand last year. Coach pokes me in the chest. "You make sure nothing distracts you this year and you'll be golden. And after three championship wins, you'll have paved your path to the Hall of Fame. A fourth would be a jar of cherries."

"I'll do my best." I run my fingers through my dark hair.

"You'll do your best." An eruption of laughter spills out of him. The man has to see how stressed I am. "Sacrifice this year, and you're football royalty. Imagine how proud you'd have made your dad."

He pats me on the back. He lets me leave after that, but he follows me out into the locker room.

"Now, Grizzlies, let's start this season with a win." Coach Stone raises his fist in the air. Most of the guys cheer and shout. "Huddle in."

He gives his speech about how everyone is watching us and how we have the opportunity to put all our names on the map. Then he slaps my back because I'm the captain and need to say something encouraging. This is usually easy for me, but today I have to clear my throat to buy myself some time.

"There's a lot of pressure out there, people are waiting to see how we look this year. Do they really need to fear us? Are we the sure bet to win again this year? We've all played a lot of football—most of us, our entire lives until now. We've won games we were supposed to lose, and we've lost games we were supposed to win. All I ask as your captain is that you leave everything you have out on that field, and I'll do the same. Now let's go!"

Damon shouts after me and gets them all going as we file out of the locker room. He's always good at riling up the team.

In the tunnel on the way out to the field, I hear my teammate Bradley talking to another player.

"She's busy a lot, but we've been able to go out a couple of times. Tomorrow night, she finally has a night off, so I'm taking her to dinner and a play."

By she, he's talking about my best friend, Ellery Wallace.

"And Coop?" the other player whispers, probably thinking that I can't hear him. I don't even have my helmet on.

"Completely fine with it." Bradley's smugness comes through in his tone.

I'm not completely fine with it. I'm not even remotely fine with it, but I don't tell Elle who she can date. We've been best friends since our junior year in college, and though I don't like the fact she's dating one of my teammates, it's not my place to stop her from living her life.

"Really. I always thought..." the other teammate whose voice I don't recognize says.

"Concentrate on the fucking game!" Damon shouts at them and walks alongside me. "Like you need to hear that shit right before a game."

I shake my head. "I'm fine. It's not like I don't know they're dating."

Damon chews on the inside of his cheek. "Of course you do." He points at the stands. "There's our number one fans."

He jogs over to three seats at the fifty-yard line. The ones where Ellery, Bryce, and Adeline all sit, except today Adeline has her and Damon's baby, Clover, with her. Clover's wearing her pink headphones and Damon's jersey. Damon lifts himself onto the ledge to kiss his daughter's cheek, and all the people around them react with awws.

"Siska! Warm the fuck up!" Coach Stone yells as if Damon is in junior high school and messing around with his friends.

My eyes catch Elle's, and my heart calms seeing her decked out in my jersey with my number written on her face with glitter. She smiles and presses her hands down in the air, telling me to calm down.

For a moment, all the anxiety making my heart pound simmers down. I've been here before. She's done that same movement in the stands before big games. I smile, thankful that she's centered me. I mouth "thank you," and her smile grows wider with the cocky look that promises she'll be telling me "I told you so" after we win this game.

It's odd to know someone so well, but there is no one else in my life I could talk to without using words and walk away feeling so heard.

"Hi, Elle!" Bradley comes up next to me, waving and interrupting us.

I glance at him on my right. He's shorter than me by a few inches, but his huge thighs are why he can race down the field and catch the ball.

"I'm not so sure I like the fact that the girl I'm dating is wearing your number," he says, his smile never fading toward her as he continues to wave.

"Well, I'm her best friend, so good luck getting that to change."

My stomach drops at the thought of coming out here one day and not seeing Elle in my jersey. She's worn my jersey since my junior year of college. Rarely does she miss any home games unless she gets called in, and even then, she makes it to part of the game a lot of times. She's my biggest fan, my biggest cheerleader, and if this douchecanoe thinks she's going to wear his jersey because he's taken her to coffee a few times, he's dead wrong.

"I think I'm going to buy her one," he says and walks away.

"What did he say?" Miles stops in front of me.

I'm guessing he's asking because my outward expression matches my inward feeling. I'm a minute away from fighting Bradley on the sidelines. I turn away from the women, not wanting Elle to see my reaction because she'll ask me later and I have no excuse.

"Bastard says Elle should be wearing his number."

She *is* dating Bradley, although it's only been a few dates and nothing remarkable from the little I've heard her discuss with the girls. I never ask. I'm not a masochist.

"Hell, Bryce didn't wear my number for a long-ass time."

I lift my eyebrow at Miles, and we both laugh. Bryce wouldn't openly do that unless she knew the relationship was going the distance.

"True," he says. "But there's no way Elle should wear Bradley's."

I want to thank Miles for having my back, but we probably sound like a bunch of high school kids trying to claim these women.

"What's the chatting about? Stop flirting with the women in the stands." Coach Stone walks by us, clipboard in hand, putting his headphones into place.

"She's my wife," Miles says, following him over to the defense side.

I say nothing as the third-string quarterback, Derek Garfield, comes over to help me warm up my arm with some throws.

By the half, we're up by one touchdown thanks to Damon's magic hands. My throw wasn't great, but he got the tips of his fingers on the ball and secured it like it was Clover in the end zone.

"Why aren't you throwing to me?" Bradley asks on our way through the tunnel.

"What are you talking about?"

"I was wide open."

I shake my head. "Did you not see my ass on the ground how many fucking times?"

He stares at me as if he's reading my mind. "You never missed me last year." Storming off, he gives me one glance back before heading into the locker room.

Since we're only up by one touchdown, the coaches scramble to decide which plays we'll run in the second half and which ones we're throwing away.

The best thing about football is how easy it is for me to push anything personal out of my mind. All that matters right now is that at the end of the game, the scoreboard says we won. That means I've done my job. So I focus on Coach Stone, then I get my team razzed to go out and fight for the win.

When the time ticks down in the fourth, we've won, but it's a long season. Coach Stone is right—I can't have any distractions this season.

CHAPTER 2

ELLERY

The ER is eerily quiet when I walk in for my shift. Passing the nurse's station, I wave and say hello, then I head into the locker room.

"Dr. Wallace," Dr. Murphy says, putting his stethoscope in the pocket of his white jacket. He's older than me, and even though he's new here, he's biding his time until someone higher up the chain leaves. He's power-hungry, and the two of us don't get along that well.

"Dr. Murphy." I turn my back to him, fiddling with the lock on my locker until it opens.

"I saw your boy's win on Sunday. Quite a game, but it must be different watching it live." I look over my shoulder to find him staring at himself in the mirror, fixing invisible strands of hair that have gone awry. "How do you get all his home games off?"

I roll my eyes because my head is buried in my locker, and he can't see me. This isn't the first time he's asked me about Cooper. It's well known that Cooper is my best friend, but usually people ask me for tickets, and that's not what he's implying.

"As soon as the schedule's out, I ask for the days off." I toe out of my gym shoes and put on the clogs I only wear in the hospital, then I take out my white coat.

"So organized. So on top of everything. Doesn't hurt that Daddy is the head of the department, right?"

I turn around and slam my locker shut. "Just say it, Clay."

He finally stops admiring himself in the mirror and faces me. "You get special treatment, and you know it."

He has no idea how many times I was reprimanded in front of the other residents about the decisions I made. I got it harder, not easier, because of who my dad is. Other residents would be told "excellent job," and I'd be told I didn't go far enough into the diagnosis.

"If you think my dad gives me special treatment, you're mistaken. You haven't been here long enough to know."

The latter part is the truth. Dr. Murphy only joined the team last year when he came to us from another hospital. The only thing he knows is that my dad heads the emergency department.

"I get the same number of days off as everyone else, and I trade shifts all the time. Hell, I'm here way more than you." I head toward the door, not in the mood to work an entire shift with him.

"Man, you're easy to rile up," he murmurs under his breath.

I stop right before opening the door and take a deep breath to stop myself from turning around and stomping back over to him. There are few people I hate in this world, but Clay Murphy is right up there at the top of my list.

I open the door, and my friend and fellow doctor, Alice, stands on the other side. "Whoa, I was just about to come get you." She must see Dr. Murphy behind me because her smile drops, and she turns away from the door. "Oh, I see."

"Something must've happened because he's back on the whole 'daddy's girl' thing again," I say under my breath as we head down the hall.

"Why does he care? I think he might like you."

I stop and stare at my friend. We became residents the same year and formed an instant friendship. At least if I have to work with Dr. Murphy today, I get to work with Alice too.

We both laugh. "We're not in the fourth grade anymore, Al. The boys shouldn't flirt by being mean."

"He seems like the type though, no?"

He walks by us, his cologne wafting behind him as if we were crop-dusted.

"That cologne is just god-awful." I cough into my elbow.

"Really? I kind of like it." She stares at his backside, and I stop at the intake desk, watching her for a moment.

"Oh my god, you like him," I whisper-shout.

How could she?

Okay, so Dr. Murphy is attractive. He has a runner's body, but the muscles in his biceps suggest he lifts weights too. His hair is always styled to perfection, and his skin has this glow to it. And… his smile is nice, although it's never pointed in my direction. I'll admit, I can see why my friend is attracted to him. Most female patients go gaga for him when they come in. A lot of the men too.

"No," she says in a way that I know means she's lying. It's the same way she denies she ate the last of the candy in our communal drawer.

"I can see it, liar."

"Funny," she says under her breath, sitting down and waiting for the physician's handover.

"Excuse me?" I sit next to her, staring at the board to see what's going on in the emergency room currently and where we'll need to pick up.

"It's just funny that you can see me crushing on Clay, but you're ignorant to your 'best friend' crushing on you."

I roll my eyes. As long as I've been friends with Cooper, I've gotten the same reaction from people—that we can't just be best friends, there has to be something that we're denying.

And honestly, it's weird to have a sex symbol for a best friend. Of course he's attractive, there's no denying it. In college, it was a tamer version of what it is now with the women and the fame. But we started to rely on one another, and soon we didn't want to lose one another. The only way to ensure he'll stay in my life for good is for him to be my best friend—not my boyfriend or my lover.

"I'm dating Bradley," I say, hoping this will shut down the direction of this conversation.

"And tell me why again?" Alice's eyebrows raise.

I want to ask her when she finds the time to do beauty rituals like wax or pluck her eyebrows. I'd like to cover mine because I'm not sure the last time I looked at my own.

"What do you mean, why?"

The smell of salami passes us, and we turn to see Hayes plop down on a chair beside me with a sandwich. "I don't want to hear it, I'm working a double tonight."

We both put up our hands.

"Hayes, why do you think Ellery is dating Bradley?" Alice asks him.

He finishes chewing. If he wasn't in a bad mood already, I'd tell him to close his mouth. "She's in denial."

They high-five one another and I groan, glancing at my watch, wondering when this shift change is happening.

"You guys just don't understand. I'm friends with Hayes, yet no one says I'm denying some deep-rooted love for him."

He puts his head on my arm and flutters his eyelids. "I'm yours whenever you're ready."

I push his head off me, and he laughs, continuing to devour his cafeteria sandwich.

"You don't go on vacation with Hayes, you don't spend holidays with him, you don't spend the night at Hayes's apartment, you don't—"

"I do those things with my other friends too. Doesn't make Cooper special."

"Are we done talking about Dr. Wallace's love life? Which Grizzly is she dating this week?" Dr. Murphy stands by the board, eyes narrowed on me.

I suck in a breath. He's such an ass.

"How about everyone stays out of my love life?" I look around at all the doctors and nurses.

My father, Dr. Wallace, doesn't say anything for a moment but nods to Dr. Mendez to start on the rounds.

"Let's walk." Dr. Mendez isn't one for getting into the personal lives of her doctors. She's all business, all of the time. Rarely jokes or cracks a smile. So I'm sure my love life is of no interest to her. "We're only at forty percent capacity right now…"

She talks while we listen.

It isn't until she stops outside a room that her eyes find me. "Mr. Euing is back. Said he was mugged, and someone hit him on the head. There's no head injury that we could see, so he's having a meal and then should be on his way." I fight the urge to go into the room, and she must notice. "Go ahead, Dr. Wallace, we've gotten nowhere with him in the past hour."

"Okay." I nod.

"See me after, and I'll let you know who else you're responsible for," Dr. Mendez says in a surprisingly nice way.

I knock on the door and enter the room. "Mr. Euing?" I say, entering the room, and then I run my hands under the sanitizer.

"There's the beauty."

I approach the bed. "How are you?" I look him over, but there's no visible sign of an altercation. He's a regular and usually finds an excuse to come in here every week or so.

"How's that big boyfriend of yours? Man, he's the talk of the town. Making Chicago look good."

I smile at him. "We've been over this. He's just my friend." I go to the computer and scan my key card to get access.

"What brought you in today? Dr. Mendez said something about a fight?"

He waves his age-spotted hand. "Tim's an asshole. He thinks he can fight me, but he can't."

I run through the bloodwork they've done on him and see that no scans were ordered since they didn't find any sign of him being concussed.

"Did this happen at a shelter?" I pull the stool over to his bedside and take a seat.

"No, he claims he owns the spot under Michigan Avenue by Nordstrom. I've been there for ages. Everyone knows that's my spot."

I sit with him for another ten minutes, get him calmed down, and tell him I'll be back. It's only a matter of time until we'll have to send him back to the streets, but at least we'll get a warm meal in him. Hopefully we won't need the bed he's in today, and I can let him stay a little longer and try to make sure he makes it to the shelter after my shift.

Eight hours later, I'm sitting at the station, looking up shelters to try to get Mr. Euing a spot, when Jennifer, our intake nurse, walks through the doors with Cooper right behind her.

"What are you doing here?" I ask him with a smile.

"I'm here to take you home."

I flick my wrist to look at my watch. It is almost time, but since I worked the second shift, it's late for him to come and get me. "You should be sleeping. You have practice in the morning."

He's dressed in his joggers and a T-shirt. His T-shirt is slightly damp, and I'm not sure if he came from a workout or if it's still humid outside.

"I'll be fine. Just saw Mr. Euing. He saw me walk by and called me in. Said you're trying to get him into a shelter tonight? Something about a fight with Tom?"

Mr. Euing *loves* Cooper. Any time he sees him here, he chats him up.

Cooper sits in a chair with his arms crossed. Compared to most of our staff, he's larger than life. Six foot four, over two hundred pounds, huge hands. He's a presence.

"Yeah. Said they got in a fight."

"I thought they were best friends." He reads my mind.

"Exactly. Something's wrong, so I really want to get him in a shelter tonight rather than be out there on the streets."

"You go finish up, and I'll call around and see if any have openings."

"Thanks. Go visit him, you know he loves you."

He stands and heads down to the room I told him.

"Jeez, he's even invested in your cases," Alice says, coming up beside me.

"Please, Mr. Euing's been coming here forever."

Just as I say that to Alice, I hear Mr. Euing shout, "Coop, my man!"

Alice shakes her head. "Everyone else gets it but you."

After she walks away, I finish doing my rounds on my patients and hand them over to the next physician.

Before I have the opportunity to go rescue Cooper, Mr. Euing walks out of his room. "I'm discharging myself," he says, proud as if he said he's been one hundred days sober. "Coop is driving me to a shelter."

"He is, is he?" I'll have to do up the paperwork to discharge him before we leave.

As they approach, Cooper leans in and whispers, "You'd never sleep otherwise. Now you'll know he's off the streets for at least one night."

This man knows me so well.

I do the discharge paperwork, and then we drive Mr. Euing to the shelter on North, drop him off, and Cooper looks at me from the driver's seat of his Land Rover.

"Thank you." I smile at him.

"I said you don't have to thank me. You wanna go for one of our drives?"

I laugh and shake my head. "It wasn't that bad of a night."

"Do it for me?" His brown eyes soak into mine.

Usually it's me who wants to drive after a bad night, so I'm a little alarmed by the sadness I see brewing in the depths of those chocolate eyes. "Of course. Anything for you."

He rolls down the windows since it's a beautiful night in Chicago and hops on Lake Shore Drive. The wind flows through my hair, and he turns up the music, allowing us to both feel as though we're escaping. Escaping what, I'm not sure.

CHAPTER 3

ELLERY

JUNIOR YEAR OF COLLEGE

was running late. I was always running late. I felt as though my body didn't know how to function unless I was running on barely any sleep and fueled on caffeine. I kept telling myself it was college, but as I steadily walked past my fellow co-eds, none of them appeared to be sweating and on the verge of passing out.

Dr. Mylard had already started his lecture when I reached the classroom. Way to make a first impression. This was my junior year, so it's not as if I had the excuse of being lost. I was surprised the lecture wasn't in an auditorium but in a small classroom of only thirty or so students. Was I even in the right class?

Trying to be discreet, I quietly shut the door, but as I turned, I noticed all the students and Dr. Mylard staring at me.

"Sorry I'm late," I said, making eye contact with him.

He smiled. "It's quite all right. Who am I to discipline a Wallace?" He signaled with his hand to take a seat.

My cheeks heated, and I walked to the only vacant seat in

the back. Sitting so far from the front usually wasn't my style, but I was thankful to be slightly hidden today. Did he have to call me out in front of everyone? Today was just one of the many times I'd hated my decision to come to this school, but my father would have it no other way. I was a Wallace, and every Wallace since this university was erected attended here.

I looked to my right and startled.

Cooper Rice was sitting beside me, and was he smiling... at me?

Everyone on campus knew Cooper Rice. He was the quarterback for our football team. Sure, my name meant something on this campus, but Cooper's name meant a whole lot more.

So much football talent, and of course, he was incredibly hot. Dark hair with eyes to match that were rimmed with thick lashes and a trim, fit body.

Dr. Mylard cleared his throat, and I turned away from Cooper's amazing dimple, unzipping my backpack to pull out my stuff. I straightened in my seat to pay attention.

"There's a syllabus online, and I suggest you follow it precisely. There is no extra credit, no retaking tests, and no makeup work. You turn in all material on time, be here on test days, and you'll have a great semester." His gaze landed on me. "If you're late, you won't."

Cooper snickered, and I glanced over before burying my head in my notebook again.

For the rest of the class, I felt Cooper looking at me, but I didn't understand why. I wasn't the type of girl football players went for. My roommate, Bryce, was always trying to get me to go out, but I wasn't the party girl. Maybe because I always felt as if my dad had eyes on me everywhere.

Cooper's type was probably the sorority girl, the girl who'd write his number on her cheeks and sit front row, pouring attention onto him about what a great player he was. They probably gave him blowjobs and didn't expect anything in return. Not that I had a lot of experience in that department.

My body was on high alert by the time Dr. Mylard ended class.

I packed up my bag, swung my backpack over my shoulder, and waited to file out of class with everyone else. Thankfully, Dr. Mylard didn't call me down to his desk, but his attention did remain on me.

Some professors respect that my ancestors helped build this campus, while others resent it and some of the board's decisions. And since I had five family members on the board, I was often looked at as enemy number one.

"Wallace!" a voice said behind me as I escaped the building and walked down the pathway back to the student center. I had an hour's break before my next class.

I stopped and looked over my shoulder, and my eyebrows shot up. Cooper Rice was jogging down the path to catch up to me?

I checked in front of me in case he was calling my cousin, who was a graduate student here. When I turned back around, I saw that some guy was fist-bumping Cooper to say hello. He kept moving until he stopped in front of me, and a group of girls all stared as they walked past.

"Hey, Coop," they said in unison. Then the judgmental eyes started on me, as if I wasn't good enough for Cooper Rice.

He waved but said nothing to them. That shouldn't make me feel good, but it did. To have a heartthrob's attention when you weren't looking for it and see him disregard other girls was a boost to the self-esteem.

"Hi," he says, putting his hand out to me. "My name is Cooper."

I laugh. "I know."

A sheepish grin filled his face, and his cheeks flushed as if he forgot how well people knew him. My attraction to him ticked up another level. "Yeah, of course."

I slid my palm into his. His callouses were the first thing I noticed, then how his bigger hand swallowed mine. "Ellery."

"Ellery."

I never thought I could get off from the way a man said my name, but now I knew that to be wrong. The sound of it instantly put me in bed with his weight over me, Cooper kissing me and whispering my name in my ear.

No wonder he had women falling at his feet.

I slid my hand out of his with a little extra pull when he didn't release it.

"Sorry." He still looked a little sheepish, and I found it endearing.

We stood there for a minute, students passing by to get to their next class, and I swear half of them patted him on the shoulder and said hello. He didn't react to any of them.

"Nice to meet you." I turned to leave, but his hand lightly cupped my elbow, stopping me.

I didn't even have to turn around because he stepped up to me. "Where are you headed?"

"Why?" I wanted to search the area for cameras. Was this some joke, Cooper Rice, giving me his attention? "I'm probably not the kind of girl you'd prefer." I continued to walk away.

"What?" he said—more to himself, I thought—and caught up to me because his legs were so damn long.

We walked up the hill from the psych building, and he wasn't fazed in the least, while I was trying to act as if I wasn't gasping for breath. I hated this hill.

"What kind of girl do I prefer?" There was laughter in his tone, and it zoomed in right between my thighs. Why was everything this man did so damn attractive?

Just then, two girls walked by. "Hey, Coop," they said in unison—again—lifting their hands and waving one finger at a time. They pushed their tits out more and scowled at me before smiling back at him and walking by, probably praying he'd check out their asses.

"Girls like that." I increased my speed to reach the student center.

"You're assuming a lot," he said. "They don't even know me. They know *of* me."

"Okay, well, I'm not sure why you're following me right now, but you should know, I'm not going to sleep with you."

"Huh, I don't remember asking."

Embarrassment heated my cheeks, but I pushed it away. "I'm just letting you know, and if you think I'm smart and can help you in that class, you're wrong. I have to take the class for my major, otherwise I wouldn't step foot in a psych building."

"You have something against psych majors? And I don't need your help to pass the class."

I stopped and stared at him for a moment.

"You're assuming a lot in this short conversation—that I'm just a dumb jock who wants as many girls as possible in his bed."

I opened my mouth and shut it. Damn him. "I just…"

He leaned in close, and that dimple in his left cheek indented further. "Assumed," he whispered, and goose bumps ran up my spine.

"I'm sorry."

"Don't be too sorry, I already did imagine you in my bed." He shrugged. "Sometimes I can't control the big guy, and he just takes over."

My mouth dropped open. "Seriously?"

He laughed. "Do you want to know the truth?"

"What's going on here? Is Cooper Rice hitting on my best friend?" Bryce approached us, her arms crossed as she took in Cooper.

"You gotta be kidding me. The girl who's been hounding

me for an interview is your best friend?" he asked me, disregarding Bryce.

"Yep."

He turned away from me and set his eyes on Bryce. "You still want that interview?"

Bryce looked at me and back at him. "Yeah."

"You got it."

"Really?" Bryce balked because Cooper had never done an interview for the school newspaper other than a quote here or there about a game.

He turned in my direction. "Come to my football game Saturday and go out with me afterward, and I'll do your friend's interview."

I balked. "You're manipulating the situation. How do you know I wouldn't have said yes if you'd just asked?"

He shrugged. "I'm trusting my gut. So?"

I looked at Bryce, who had her hands in front of her in a prayer pose. She'd kept me up late at night before going on about how much she wanted an interview with Cooper. And seriously, a night out with Cooper wouldn't be so bad, I guess.

"Fine, do the interview with Bryce and you have a deal."

His smile only widened, and I saw then that he had two dimples. He ran his hand through his dark hair. "Got it."

Bryce raised her hand. "Excuse me?"

I ignored her. She'd pretend to be put out, but she loved football players. She'd probably marry one someday.

Cooper leaned into my personal space. "Saturday it is. Tickets will be at will-call, and meet me afterward where all the players leave from. Bryce will show you."

My heart beat rapidly. What did I just get myself into?

CHAPTER 4

COOPER

We have Tuesdays off, and while I love when my day off is the same as Ellery's, lately we haven't spent them together. She's been with Bradley on one of his lame dates. But today, it's the annual flu shot rollout at the hospital. From the very first year Ellery took part, I've been the guy who gets the first shot to show kids—and some of the adults—that there's nothing to be afraid of.

I head up to the big room in the hospital that houses the flu shot clinic every year and see the cameras. The press is interviewing someone who I'm sure is a doctor or a nurse. Since they're distracted, I look around the room to find Ellery.

"Cooper?"

That voice still scares the crap out of me even though I've known him for years. I turn, and his hand is already extended toward me.

"Good morning, Mr. Wallace."

Elle's dad's hair is thinner than the last time I saw him. "Thank you for coming. I know this cause is a big one for Ellery."

"I'd be nowhere else."

He smiles. There's something behind it I can't decipher, but he's thinking for sure. "You're a good friend to her."

"She is to me too."

If he knew how much I imagine his daughter inappropriately, he might not be so complimentary.

"Well, let's get this show on the road. You're the front man, let's go find our girl." He claps me on the back.

Mr. Wallace has always been kind to me, but maybe that's because I've only been presented to him as being in the friend zone. He brags about me to his friends. I've overheard him at parties. "My daughter is best friends with Cooper Rice. He's a great guy. Gets us tickets whenever we want. Sure, I'll take you sometime."

Her mom makes me my favorite meals and spoils me like my mom never had time to do.

Ellery comes out from a room in the back, smiling when she sees me and looks at her watch. "Right on time." Then she approaches her dad and hugs him and gives him a kiss on the cheek. "Hi, Dad, thank you for being here."

"Miss my baby girl's shining moment? Never."

She hugs me, and I hold her a little tighter than normal. I've been missing her since she started dating Bradley. Her usual fruity-scented shampoo has me inhaling a second time. She pulls away faster than I want, but who am I to complain? She's not mine.

"Let's go get that shot, big guy." She walks ahead.

Her dad's eyebrows are scrunched as he looks at me. I ignore him and follow her to a station where cameras are already set up. But there's a commotion over by the door. When the crowd clears, I spot Bradley with his hands in his pockets, answering questions.

What the hell is he doing here?

"Oh," Ellery says.

He spots her and breaks the distance, the press following him. "I hope you don't mind, but you mentioned attendance being low last year and thought maybe two Grizzlies might help drive more people in." He glances in my direction. "What's up, Coop?" He holds out his fist to bump mine, and I do, though reluctantly.

"Bradley," I say with a nod.

"I don't think we've met." Mr. Wallace approaches Bradley with his hand out.

"Oh, Dad, this is Bradley. Bradley, this is my dad." Ellery's eyes find mine because if we'd wanted more Grizzlies, I would've asked my best buds, the MVPs from the past two years, Miles and Damon.

Bradley talks to Mr. Wallace as though they've been friends forever, telling him how he'll score him some tickets to a game. Mr. Wallace looks at me, then back at Bradley.

I liked the guy and respected him for asking me if he could date Elle, but now that it actually seems as though it might become something, I'm starting to lose my shit. He's treading on my territory.

"I heard you were coming over for dinner tonight." Mr. Wallace says to Bradley.

I clear my throat, and Elle's eyes find mine again.

"Mom insisted," she mouths.

"I'm eager to meet the other half of the couple who made such a great daughter." Bradley puts his arm around Elle's shoulders.

I turn around to be anywhere but here, running right into a nurse. *Fuck*.

"Jeez, I'm sorry." I squat to help her pick up the boxes of Band-Aids she dropped.

"It's okay. Cooper Rice can run into me anytime." She laughs. "God, did that sound as lame as it did when I heard it back in my head?"

She's younger than me, probably in her early twenties, and her flush is cute, but the flirting isn't doing much for me.

"I'm Jewel."

"Nice to meet you, Jewel. I guess you already know who I am."

We both stand, and I hand her the boxes I picked up. "Of course, and don't worry, it isn't me giving you your shot today."

I laugh. "It's okay, I bumped into you."

A few cameras snap some pictures, and Jewel looks over at them. Welcome to the gossip column, Jewel.

I lean forward and whisper in her ear, "Hide your nametag until they're gone."

Her eyes widen as if a bear is behind her, ready to kill.

The gossip blogs and those who read them will likely shred her like a bear if they find out who she is. So many women are so protective of me, though they don't even know me. Jewel is innocent and doesn't need to be brought into it.

"Are you guys ready?" Elle comes over and looks at Jewel for a moment before smiling. "Thank you for grabbing more." She helps Jewel put the boxes on the table with the rest of the extra supplies.

"Okay, we need two chairs. Should we put them next to one another?" a woman who works for the hospital asks as they reconfigure how they're going to get Bradley and me in the photo.

I'm more than aggravated at this point.

"I don't want it in my right, that's my dominant arm," Bradley says.

"Well, I can't get it in my right, it's my throwing arm," I counter.

"We'll just have to put someone between them," someone suggests.

A woman I recognize from years past as being the PR rep for the hospital appears from nowhere to tell us her opinion. "And lose this great shot? No way. These two side-by-side will sell the public on getting their flu shot."

I'm not budging. There's no way I'm gonna play with a sore arm.

"It shouldn't be sore more than a couple days," Ellery says.

Neither of us says a word.

She gives me "the look." The one that usually gets me to do just about anything for her. But not this time. Let Dreamboy take the hit—he's the one getting all the benefits.

I run my hand down my face because I don't think like this. At least I never used to. I'm way more upset about this relationship than I should be.

"I'll get it in my right." Bradley smiles as though he just disarmed a bomb and saved us. Get a grip, you're a football player.

We sit in the chairs, a nurse on either side of us as the cameras and video people all get their shots. The nurses inject us, and neither of us flinches.

Ellery gets in front of the cameras, standing right in front of us. She's wearing her white coat and long pants with the clogs she loves so much. One Christmas, I gave her clogs with my number on them, but I rarely see her wear them.

"And it's as simple as that. Just a moment of your time to protect you and those you love from the flu virus this season."

The nurse puts the Band-Aid on me as Ellery finishes. Then they open the doors and the public files in, picking up clipboards to fill out paperwork.

Bradley seeks out Ellery, but she's busy, and he's only going to piss her off. I learned that year one. I make my way around all the stations, saying hello, signing some autographs, and snapping selfies with people while making sure to show the sticker on my shirt that says I got my flu shot. Hopefully the more pictures that are shared, the more it will remind people to get the shot themselves.

Eventually, Bradley discovers what I could have told him—Ellery has no time for him.

"So, what do you do now?" he asks, looking around.

"You just socialize. She's done in a few hours." I shrug.

"Really? That long? I figured she'd start this off and be done, have others be in charge."

I look at him pointedly. "How many dates have you been on with her?"

"More than you."

I raise my eyebrows, and he laughs, knocking his shoulder into mine. *Fucker*.

"I'm kidding. Seriously, it's intimidating how well you two know one another," he says. "If I have to hear one more time, 'Cooper and I…' I'm going to go berserk."

"We've been friends for a very long time."

"And you do everything together from the sound of it."

I should not be enjoying his jealousy, but I am. Maybe that makes me a petty man, but I don't care. I'm happy to hear my name comes up often in their conversations. It means she's not forgetting about me.

"When we have time, we do stuff together. She's really busy." Am I being a dick by giving him reasons why it might not work with them? Probably, but I find it hard to stop myself.

"I figured that one out the first time I asked her on a date. She's hard to nail down. We've been on one official date, and the rest have been coffee or lunch dates." He sounds displeased.

"She loves her job."

"So do I, but shit." He crosses his arms.

I notice a kid refusing to get a shot at one of the stations. His mom is trying to coax him into it.

"Just remember how much off time we get through the year. She's doing this year-round." I walk away from Bradley and squat next to the kid. I'm not sure he knows who I am.

The six-year-old's blond mop of hair lands right above his bright blue eyes filled with unshed tears.

"Do you like football?" I ask.

He shrugs.

I pick up the bin each station has with prize packs for the little kids. "Want to pick one of these?"

"What about Superman? You like him?" Bradley squats next to me.

I glance over my shoulder. What the fuck is he doing? Find your own kid, asshole.

The boy nods.

"Iron Man? Captain America?" Bradley keeps it up, and the kid's eyes grow more excited with each superhero he rhymes off.

"Yeah," the little boy says, eyes no longer filled with tears.

"They're not afraid of the shots, and neither should you be," Bradley says.

The mom and nurse smile at Bradley, and I want to punch him in the fucking nose.

"No shot!" The boy's excitement is wiped clean from his face.

I show him the prize bin again. "You can get anything in here after you get your shot."

The kid looks at the bin, his hand digging in. He lifts out a football. My kind of kid. But he quickly drops it and picks up a puzzle thing. Whatever he wants.

"That's what you want?" I ask.

He nods.

"All right, now be really brave, and if you have to, close your eyes and imagine playing with the puzzle."

The nurse wipes down the spot and gives him the shot.

"Are your eyes shut really tight?"

He nods.

"Okay…" I lean closer to him. "You're done," I whisper.

His blue eyes pop open, and his mouth hangs open. "Really?"

I hand him the puzzle. "Really. You're very brave."

He looks at his mom. "I didn't feel it."

She mouths "Thank you," and I nod.

"I see you're working your magic again this year," Ellery says, coming over between us.

Bradley and I stand, him moving closer to her, and I refrain from growling like a guard dog.

"Cooper's known for putting the kids at ease," she tells Bradley.

And just like that, someone calls me over to their booth.

"Gotta go where I'm needed." I wink.

Bradley shoots me a look that says "whatever" while Ellery smiles, completely oblivious to the fact that both of us want her—even if only one of us should.

CHAPTER 5

ELLERY

"So, you're bringing Bradley to Peeper's Alley?" Bryce asks while we're waiting for the guys to come out onto the field, her gaze diverting to Adeline.

"Um... yeah, why?"

Bryce shrugs, but it doesn't seem like she was just wondering. She's judging.

"Since when are you at a loss for words?" I ask.

"We just don't normally invite other people."

"Isn't that because two of us three are dating players? Cooper is welcome to bring someone. Heck, after game day, he can grab any available woman hanging out to get a pic and bring her into the back room if he wants." I grab my popcorn and shove it in my mouth.

Neither of them says anything, and I get it. Me dating Bradley has rocked the boat in this glorious six-person friendship. But it was bound to happen at some point. It just never has happened until now. Neither Cooper nor I have ever brought the person we're dating around each other, but I can't help that they're teammates. Neither of us has found anything serious since we came into one another's lives back in college.

"And Cooper knows?"

"Oh, I didn't know he gets to police who I can and cannot bring."

Bryce is annoying me, and the game hasn't even started yet. The seats next to me fill, and we have to lower our voices.

Bryce says, "I didn't mean it like that. It's just… weird."

"Well, I'm sorry you're not comfortable."

"Jeez, Elle, I was just conveying my feelings." She turns her body away from me and sips her beer.

Adeline pretends she has to get something out of the diaper bag while Clover is dancing on her lap to the music. The Grizzlies are announced and come out onto the field as the crowd roars. Clover leans to look over toward the tunnel with her pacifier in her mouth.

I'm just happy I don't have to talk about Cooper anymore.

I'm not sure what Bryce expects me to do. We've been over this. He and I will never be a couple. Sure, our relationship isn't in sibling territory, but we don't want to lose one another, and we promised each other that a long time ago. And it's not as if Cooper has given me any indication that he wants to change anything.

Damon jogs over, and Clover claps, smiling around her pacifier. It might be the cutest thing I've ever seen, and for a moment, I wonder what it would be like to have a little one like her. How would Cooper be as a dad? He's a great uncle figure to Clover.

As usual, Damon plays with fire as he lifts himself up on the ledge and wraps his arms around Adeline, squeezing Clover between them. His lips find Adeline's, and the people around us all squeal with joy.

"Always making fans," I say.

"Good luck," Adeline says. "Wish Daddy good luck."

Damon pushes his finger gently into Clover's stomach. "Tell Mommy that Daddy doesn't need luck."

"There's the cocky side we all love," Bryce says, rolling her eyes.

"Don't do that, Bryce," Damon says without looking away from his wife and child.

God, that look in his eye, like he'd like to defer the game and sit in the stands with them. What must it be like to have a man look at you like that?

I'm so transfixed by them that Bryce has to elbow me to wave to Bradley.

"Thanks. It's just so…"

"Toothache inducing? Yup." Bryce sips some more beer. She blows a kiss to Miles, who brings up both hands and forms a heart.

After I wave to Bradley, my eyes search out Cooper, but he's already talking to his coach about the plays, and it looks as though he's about to warm up his arm.

"Jesus Christ!" Coach Stone yells. "I get it that you love your family, but get down and warm up, Siska!"

Damon smiles and kisses Adeline one last time before kissing Clover's cheek. He whispers something only Adeline can hear, but she blushes as he jumps down.

"Dada!" Clover yells.

He turns around, blowing her a kiss. Her bottom lip quivers and Adeline reaches into the bag, grabbing a snack to distract Clover, but her eyes are fixated on her dad.

"What did he say to you?" Bryce asks because she thinks everything is her business.

"Nothing." She shakes her head, but she can't get the smile off her face, nor can she stop blushing.

"OMG, what?" Bryce asks again.

Adeline looks around, then leans in closer to us. "If he scores two touchdowns and they win, I promised him we'd go away for a weekend during the bye week, just the two of us."

"How come I don't think that's all of it?" Bryce smirks.

Adeline's cheeks grow pinker, and she strips her gaze away from us.

"Okay, keep the dirty stuff between you two, but let me watch Clover while you're gone," Bryce says.

"Oh, you'd want to do that?" Adeline asks.

"Of course."

I stare at Bryce. Since when does she volunteer to babysit? I mean, we all love Clover, but a whole weekend with Clover?

"Okay, I guess we'll see what happens today." Adeline suddenly looks as if she doesn't want Damon to score two touchdowns, which we all know is feasible.

"Clover, come to Auntie Bryce." Bryce holds out her hands, her diamond rings looking as though she just got them cleaned as they sparkle so brightly.

Clover goes of course, because she pretty easily goes to all of us. Bryce sits the baby on her lap and talks to her as if Clover is six, pointing out players and saying how we don't like the green team, only the orange and blue one.

Adeline sits back and, for the first time since we got here, takes a sip of her soft drink, watching the guys warm up.

"What's it like?" I ask her.

"What?" Her head tilts.

"Marriage? Kids?"

She laughs. "Hectic. But nothing really changed after we got married."

Bryce and Miles were married in a big ceremony over the summer, and right after, Damon and Adeline rushed off to Vegas to tie the knot, deciding they didn't want any part of a big wedding for themselves.

"It has to be more than just hectic. You're too happy for hectic."

"True. I'm not sure how to explain it. For me, it's like peace. Although our life is crazy, there's something about knowing someone else out there loves your daughter as much as you, and you just as much as you love him. I know we're in the early days for the love thing, but I can't imagine not wanting to spend every minute with Damon and Clover."

I smile, remembering that feeling when I first met Cooper. Thank goodness our psych class was three times a week. Tuesdays and Thursdays dragged until we got to the point where we were hanging out then too.

"You've felt it before?" Adeline studies me.

I shrug and drink my water, bringing my popcorn back to my lap. I'm not saying a word. Admitting I had feelings for my best friend would only further the commentary that there's something going on with Cooper and me. But that was so long ago. It's hilarious to think of us being together now.

"Bradley?" she asks, and I want to thank her for giving me a reprieve on the whole "you love Cooper" thing. Adeline is the sweetest person I've ever known.

"No."

She gives me a small grin. "I didn't think so."

We don't wait for the guys at the stadium after the game. Instead, we head to Peeper's Alley bar. When we get out of the car that Damon hired for Adeline and Clover, there's a crowd around Peeper's Alley, most women wearing our men's jerseys.

"This is always kind of awkward, no?" Adeline says.

"Only to you. I like to show off to them that my man is taken, and they're not sinking their teeth into him." Bryce saunters out of the vehicle and winds her way toward the entrance.

"I want to be her someday," Adeline says, holding a sleeping Clover to her chest.

I laugh. "I'll grab the car seat."

After seeing Bryce, the women turn around, and the whispers commence. We walk through a group of women, but one of them reaches for my arm and throws me back.

"No cuts," she says.

I scowl at her. "Excuse me? I'm expected in there."

"Oh please." The woman looks drunk, and of course she's wearing Cooper's jersey, matching mine. "If you think you're getting in there before me because you look like the cheerleader type—"

"I'm friends with him."

"It's her, the best friend," another girl yells.

"Ellery!" Adeline calls from the door.

"I'm fine. Go." I wave her off, wanting, for some reason, to finish this.

"You're best friends. Are you a lesbian?" the woman asks me.

Here we go.

"No, I'm not."

"Then I don't buy it." She looks as if she wants to spit in my face.

Her friend steps in, trying to get her to keep quiet. "Just excuse her, she's had a lot to drink tonight."

The group goes wild, and I look around and spot Damon and Miles going in the back entrance of the bar, which is what we should've done. But that would have meant Adeline and Clover had to go through the basement and up the flight of stairs to enter Peeper's. Ruby isn't a fan of us using that entrance except for days like this. I used it once with Cooper when his fame skyrocketed from all his endorsements two years ago.

"Excuse us." Cooper pops up beside me and takes the car seat in one hand and grabs my hand with the other, weaving us through the crowd.

They all yell his name. I keep my head down as we enter, and he leads us to the back room.

"What were you doing?" he asks once we're secure.

Damon and Miles come through the other door, Damon beelining it over to Adeline.

"I think that was two touchdowns, baby." He holds up two fingers and does a dance as he gets closer.

"You wake her, and she's yours for the rest of the night," Adeline says.

He stops mid-stride and walks over more slowly, then puts his arm around her shoulders and kisses her temple as they both stare at their baby.

"Hey, I think you left one out there. He's all caught up with those women." Ruby, who owns the bar, brings in a few pitchers of beer.

"Shit, Bradley," I say.

Cooper steps away from me and goes to fill his beer mug.

"I'll be right back," I say.

I go out to the main part of the bar and ask Ruby to fetch Bradley from the grips of those starved women.

She does, and when Bradley sees me, he looks back over his shoulder at the chaos outside. "Crazy. Do they get like this all the time?"

"After every home game for the most part." I shrug.

As I lead him to the back room, he continues to look over his shoulder. "Amazing. Damn."

I want to ask if he'd prefer to be out there with all those girls, but I don't know if I want the answer.

I bring him into the private room where the guys are arguing about plays. Bryce is practically taking mommy classes from Adeline. I think I need to have a chat with Bryce later.

Bradley quickly joins the guys. I go over to the ladies and realize that I missed that there's a woman sitting next to Cooper. Who the hell is she? She's so close to him that she definitely came with him. What the hell?

"She came in, like, a minute ago. Ruby started screaming when she came through the basement, telling her to go away, and Cooper said she was with him," Bryce tells me under her breath.

"Oh."

She's cute. Blonde like he likes and light eyes. She's petite though. Maybe he likes them small, not tall for a woman like me.

"Who is she?" I ask.

Bryce shrugs.

"He met her at the grocery store. I guess she didn't know who he was. Sounds a little unbelievable to me." Adeline rolls her eyes.

As the night goes on, I try not to pay much attention to Cooper and his date, but I can't help it. He's attentive to her like he usually is with me. Bradley seems to prefer hanging with the guys and talking post-game stuff, even while Damon holds Clover while she sleeps.

Cooper and his girl play darts. She pretends she sucks so he has to lean over her to give her lessons. Give me a break, who does this girl think she's fooling?

He waits until the night is halfway done before joining us all at the table again. "Hey, Elle, I don't think you've met Maya yet. Maya, this is Ellery."

She smiles and says, "Nice to meet you."

"You too." Although I don't mean it. I much preferred it when we kept boyfriends and girlfriends out of our friendship.

My phone rings and I pull it out. When I see that it's the hospital, I'm thankful I'm being called in.

"Gotta go. Sorry," I whisper to Bradley.

"You got called in? Now?" His tone tells me he's annoyed, though I don't know why. He spent the majority of the night talking with the guys.

"Yeah."

I wait for a beat, but he doesn't offer to walk me out, so I say my goodbyes, and Bradley says he'll call me tomorrow.

When I get outside, I inhale a deep breath, but before I can hail a taxi, a hand finds mine. I look over to see Cooper.

"Your boyfriend should know that you need to be walked out of here." He holds his hand out for a taxi coming down the street, and it pulls over in front of us. "I hope it's nothing serious." He opens the taxi door and waits for me to get in.

"Thank you," I say.

A small smile creases Cooper's lips. "I'll always take care of you. You know that."

The taxi pulls away from the curb, and I lean back in the seat.

What was all that tonight? Surely it wasn't jealousy. No way.

It's just that things are changing between Cooper and me, and change is always hard. I'll get used to it. We both will.

CHAPTER 6
COOPER

JUNIOR YEAR OF COLLEGE

I was in the tunnel, waiting for our team to be called onto the field. Usually I was pretty quiet, but that day, I was even more so because I was nervous that when I looked into the stands, Ellery wouldn't be there. Giving her an ultimatum like that had been a dick move, but I'd known she'd agree to a date for her friend.

And why was I so interested in Ellery Wallace? I wasn't even sure. She was hot, there was no doubt about that. But every day a new girl hit on me, gave me her phone number, or openly flirted with me, and there I was, fixated on a girl who didn't see me like that from what she said. I called her bullshit though. She liked what she saw, the same as I did her.

When they finally announced us, we all ran onto the field, fists pumping. Some guys jumped and slammed against each other to get hyped, but I looked in the stands. I'd gotten her the good tickets, away from the student area.

I bit down on my smile when I saw her with Bryce at the fifty-yard line. But Ellery was sitting next to my parents. They hadn't informed me they were coming up until I'd already made the arrangements, so I was sure it was awkward for her.

Our eyes locked, and I waved to the group, earning four waves back, plus someone from a few rows up who must've thought I knew them.

From there, I concentrated on the game and pushed away the fact that not only was my hero, my dad, there, but so was the girl I couldn't stop thinking about.

We were behind at the half, and as I was about to head into the locker room for the quick break, my dad called out to me. Of course he'd gotten through security—he was Tom Rice, a Hall of Fame quarterback. I looked a lot like him, except for my eyes. Those came from my mom.

"You gotta be faster out of the pocket," he said. "Your O-line is doing an okay job, but use those instincts." He tapped my temple.

I nodded, never refusing my dad's advice.

"Does this have anything to do with the girl sitting next to your mom?"

"No." I shook my head.

"We've been over this. No girlfriends in college. It'll only distract you, and that will cost you later."

"She's just a friend." I lied because my dad didn't need to know the truth.

My mom had been his high school sweetheart, and he'd still made it to the pros. Of course, that was when things got crazy for them, which was part of what had scared me about having someone special in my life.

"Good." He smiled, but it was the creepy one he had when he talked about women. One that made me think maybe my mom had reason to be worried about all those out-of-town games and boys' vacations.

"I gotta go." I looked back at the door of the locker room.

"Yeah, go. Just remember, faster out of the pocket and look

downfield. You have the best arm in the league. Fucking use it." He turned and walked away.

My cleats clicked on the cement as I finished my walk to the locker room.

"Where the hell have you been, Rice?" Coach yelled.

"Sorry, my dad wanted a word."

Coach's face softened, and he rushed me over to where the rest of the offensive line was going over the new plays. Coach told me the same as my dad, that I wasn't getting out of the pocket fast enough, and he told my O-line to win me some more time by blocking properly.

On the way back out, I glanced at the stands and saw Ellery laughing at something my mom was saying. My dad was talking to the guy next to him, and when he pointed at me, I stripped my gaze away.

In the end, we won by only one touchdown. Maybe I'd been distracted, but it was hard to say by whom, my dad or Ellery.

I showered and got dressed. I'd been invited to the parties all my teammates were going to, but I had to go to dinner with my parents, which put a wrench in my plans with Ellery.

When I walked out there, the usual congregation of students congratulated us. I fist-pumped and gave them a high-five on my way through the group. A girl jumped into my arms, leaving me no choice but to catch her with my hands on her ass. She surprised me by kissing my cheek and telling me congratulations. The smell of alcohol on her breath could've gotten me drunk.

I finally made it to Ellery, who looked incredibly uncomfortable with the whole scene. Bryce sat on a cement ledge, uncaring because she'd witnessed this after trying to get us for interviews and one-liners for the newspaper.

"Hey," I said to them.

Bryce hopped off the cement ledge.

"Congratulations," Ellery said.

"Congrats, Cooper," Bryce echoed.

"Thanks. Hey, I'm sorry about my parents. Last minute they decided to come and…"

"You didn't want to put off this date with Ellery," Bryce finished for me.

My head whipped in her direction, and she laughed.

"You're not wrong. But now I have to go to dinner with my parents." I sighed.

"No worries, we got invited. And if you think we're going to pass up the best restaurant in town, you're crazy," Bryce said, but I wanted to know what Ellery thought.

"Excuse us for a minute," I said and gently took Ellery's elbow, leading her away from her best friend. "Are you sure you're okay with this? It wasn't my intention that you'd meet my parents, let alone sit through an entire game with them, on top of dinner."

I couldn't imagine the things she had probably heard from my dad in those stands, but I'd never ask.

"It's okay, and we already accepted the dinner invitation, but if you'd rather we not go, I understand. This whole thing is a little awkward." She gave me a small smile.

"No, I'd love for you to come." I probably sounded too enthusiastic.

But she smiled at me and said, "Okay then, let's go."

———

A half hour later, we were at the restaurant where my parents were waiting for us. We sat down, Ellery next to my mom and Bryce next to my father so I could sit next to Ellery. For a second, Bryce tried to make it seem like she was going to sit between us, and that would not have been okay. I'd waited all week for tonight, and I wasn't going to be cockblocked by Bryce *and* my parents.

We ordered, each of us getting a steak since my dad would only take us to a steakhouse.

"So, tell me about yourself, Ellery?" my dad asked.

I straightened. I knew he was baiting her to see if the friendship remark I made was true.

I loved my dad, and he'd been a pillar in my life. Taught me everything about being the quarterback I was. We'd rebuilt cars, including a Corvette that sat in their garage waiting for me to graduate from college. I'd always gone to him for advice, and I was in agreement with him about waiting until I'd gone pro to find a girlfriend, but I didn't appreciate him sticking his nose in here.

He always said he wasn't asking me not to sleep with girls, just not to commit, but that wasn't the type of guy I was. I wanted the connection, the respect, and the love for one another. Maybe that was the product of my mom raising me since she was the one who was always home.

"I'm a pre-med student," Ellery said.

"Really?" I asked because I didn't know, and it was impressive.

"I thought you two were friends?" My dad wagged his finger between us.

Ellery turned her head toward me and tilted it. Bryce coughed, almost spitting out her water.

"We're new friends," I answered.

"Wallace is a name with some clout around this school. Are you related?" my dad asked.

"The girl doesn't want the third degree."

My mom tried to intervene, but we both knew whatever or whoever my dad felt was a threat to me making it pro, he made it his business. And when I say pro, I mean I had to be drafted within the first five picks for him to be happy.

"I am." She nodded.

I'd figured from Dr. Mylard's comment when she was late

to class that she was related to the Wallace family buildings I saw everywhere on campus.

"So, I'm sure your parents have high hopes for your success, just like we have with Cooper."

Fuck. Seriously, he was going to do this right now?

"My father, yes. He'd like me to follow in his footsteps and become an emergency room doctor," Ellery said.

"And a boyfriend would distract you from achieving that, no?" My dad arched an eyebrow.

"Dad…" I groaned, but he cut me a look.

"My parents never said anything like that, but I have a long road ahead of me. Having a boyfriend in medical school is near impossible." She looked at me from the corner of her eye, almost apologetic.

"Your parents are smart. You two are young, so I'm glad to hear it's only friendship between the two of you."

My heart felt as if it had been pummeled as I watched Ellery take her water cup and drink down a big gulp.

"For sure," she managed to squeeze out afterward.

Our meals arrived, and we all dug in. There was hardly any more conversation at the table except for my dad giving his play-by-play feedback on my performance on the field. Talk about embarrassing. Hadn't my dad ever heard of private family conversations?

By the time my mom and dad dropped Ellery and Bryce off at their apartment, I couldn't even walk them up to the door because my dad wanted me to accompany them to their hotel to go over more stuff from the game.

I wasn't stupid though. It was his way of controlling me, making sure I fell in line. And as always, I did.

CHAPTER 7
ELLERY

"I'm not sure how he's going to feel about you coming," I say to Bradley as we sit in the backseat of an Uber on our way to the location of Cooper's endorsement deal.

"I haven't scored an endorsement yet, so I figured if I knew how one worked, I'd be ahead of the game. Plus, I'm sure the captain of the team would love to help a newbie."

He has a point. Cooper is always willing to help the guys on the team. More than once, he's cut our time short or we've been interrupted so he could help teammates find an apartment, take them to lunch to give them some advice, or for a million other reasons. He takes the title of captain seriously. Maybe I'm just not sure where Cooper stands on me dating Bradley. Lately he's been weird about it.

We exit the Uber, and Bradley secures his hand around mine as we cross the street to the address that Cooper gave me. He should be done soon, and we're going to lunch afterward.

I knock on the door, and a security guy opens it. After showing identification, we're allowed in. Bradley fist bumps the security guard as though he knows him, introducing himself by telling the guard he's the wide receiver for the Grizzlies.

Bradley is the opposite of Cooper, but at the same time, he's been sweet to me. I'm just used to Cooper is all. I mean, we have an almost ten-year friendship of being glued to each other's sides.

"Great, Cooper, pretend you're throwing," someone says in the photo shoot area.

When we reach it, sure enough, Cooper is dressed in joggers and a crisp T-shirt in front of a green screen pretending to throw a football, smiling at no one. Those dimples that hooked me from the first time we met are prominent. It's unfair that he's as good at football as he is good-looking. The universe should have gifted one or the other.

His agent, Jagger, stands to the side. He's dressed in a perfectly pressed suit that fits him like a glove. The man is attractive, and he knows it. Thankfully, he also loves his wife and kids. So much so that he doesn't always attend these kinds of things.

I place my hand on Jagger's shoulder, and he turns, his face lighting up in a genuine smile. "Elle!" He wraps his arms around me, pulling me into him.

"How is the family?" I ask when we separate.

Bradley steps next to me with a stack of cookies in his hand. Guess he found the craft services table.

"Great. I forced them here on vacation. My son is in agony without his game console." He laughs as though he enjoys tormenting his son.

"Oh, we should've done dinner. I have Quinn's latest on my e-reader, but it's been crazy at work. Tell her I've converted the entire Mercy Hospital staff into her fans."

He beams. "Oh, she'll love that. I mean, it's easy to write all those awesome romance stories when you have a real-life hero like me as your husband." He puffs out his chest.

I laugh. "I'm sure she'd agree with you."

He laughs even harder, and it interrupts the photo shoot. Everyone working on the set turns toward us.

"Sorry," I whisper.

Jagger backs up, and I find Cooper staring at Bradley. Bradley's too busy eating his cookies and looking around as though he's a little kid at the North Pole.

When I first started dating Bradley, I wasn't prepared for how much he loves fame. He never shies away from being recognized, and he practically announces who he is when we go places.

I guess whatever was working isn't now that we've interrupted them, so the photographer calls a five-minute break, telling Cooper he needs to change into his next outfit. Cooper holds up his hand to tell them in a second and heads in our direction.

When I hug him, he barely hugs me back.

"I thought it was just you coming," Cooper says, and I can tell from his tone that he's not happy.

"Sorry, he said he hasn't scored an endorsement deal yet and wanted to know what it was like."

"Nice excuse," he says so softly that I'm not sure he wanted me to hear him. Cooper greets Bradley and puts his hand out, but they end up having to bump elbows because Bradley's hands are still full of food.

"Man, this is awesome." Bradley doesn't actually say hello or thank Cooper for not telling him to get out. "And you do how many of these?"

Jagger eyes me and nods toward Bradley as if asking "Who is this guy?" I'm not super surprised. I mean, Jagger represents top-tier athletes—for example, Cooper. Bradley is just coming up and hasn't really made a name for himself yet.

"Jagger Kale?" Bradley's mouth hangs open. Did he really just notice him?

"Hey, man. Bradley Powers, right?" Jagger says. I guess he does know him.

Bradley's eyebrows shoot up. "You know me?"

"It's my business to know you. Thanks for making our man look so good last game." Jagger puts his hand on Cooper's shoulder and squeezes.

"I make myself look good," Cooper says. "Hey, want to come with me for a second?" he asks me.

Bradley and Jagger are now in a conversation about how Bradley can get one of these endorsement deals and Jagger is asking who his agent is, so I sneak off.

Once we're in the hallway, Cooper takes my hand and leads me to his changing room. The door shuts, and he stands with his back against the door while I look around the space.

"What's wrong with you?" I ask.

"Nothing. I just…" He shakes his head. "Nothing. So what does this mean for lunch? Another threesome like breakfast the other day after the flu shot drive?"

I sit in his makeup chair, spinning around as if I'm five years old. "I thought you liked him?"

He moves his hand up to run it through his hair but stops, knowing he can't mess it up. "I do, it's just… I never get you alone anymore."

I try not to smile but fail miserably.

There's a knock on the door. Cooper opens the door and a woman in her forties flies through. She's got short red hair, black-rimmed glasses, and probably weighs not much more than a hundred pounds.

"Here's the wardrobe for the next set of shots." She hands him a small piece of clothing.

Cooper looks at it, then unfolds it to show a pair of boxer briefs. "What is this?"

"The new line. Didn't they tell you when they booked you?" the woman asks before leaving.

"Jagger!" Cooper shouts.

Jagger joins us in the room, Bradley in tow. "What's up?"

Cooper holds up the briefs. "Since when do I model underwear?"

"Since the people paying you are expanding their brand. We discussed this on the way here, and you said you were up for whatever."

"Excuse me." The little red-haired woman peeks her head in the door. She points at me. "Can I talk to you?"

"Sure."

I walk out, everyone watching me and looking as confused as I feel. I'm assuming she's just going to ask me to win Cooper over about the underwear.

"I'm sorry he's being difficult. He'll make up his mind and—"

"Have you ever modeled?" she asks, interrupting me.

I laugh. "Modeled? Um… no. Unless you count the candid picture in my university medical program brochure, and if you'd seen it, you'd know that I do not photograph well."

"The model we had set up today to shoot with Cooper had to fly home to a sick relative unexpectedly this morning. And the clients are eager to get this new line of underwear out."

My eyes widen. "I'm sorry, I am not going to model in my underwear."

"You won't be just standing there. There's a robe for you to walk out on set in, and you'll be under the covers beside Cooper. I thought since he wasn't thrilled about it, maybe doing it with his girlfriend would make him more comfortable."

I chuckle. "I'm not his girlfriend. Just a friend."

"*Best* friend, and Jagger says I have no choice but to do this." Cooper, who must have been eavesdropping, walks over to us. "Please, Elle."

The red-haired woman smiles at me, probably thinking his magic dimples will do the trick.

"Do you have any idea what you're asking of me?" I cross my arms.

"I'll give you two a minute, but just in case, you're all set up in that dressing room." She points at the one next to Cooper's.

I shake my head violently, but Cooper takes my hands. "I just want this over with, and if I have to do an underwear photo shoot, I'd rather it be with you."

I ignore the way my tummy feels fuzzy when he says that.

"I want the Corvette," I say, knowing he'd never give me the car he rebuilt with his dad. I don't really want it, but I want him to understand how big a favor he's asking.

"*No* fucking way. Ask for something else."

I think long and hard. "A vacation then. Beach. Privacy."

He nods. "Done."

I knew he'd say yes.

"I better be getting paid for this," I mumble and go into the dressing room, slamming the door like a true diva.

Someone knocks on the door after I've dressed. Thank goodness I shaved this morning. How horrendous would that have been?

I open the door a sliver.

"Ready?" Cooper has a robe on, and suddenly this all seems way too real.

"What am I doing? I am not a model," I whisper to him.

He slithers through the opening, and I shut the door after him.

"I'm not a model either," Cooper says.

"No, but you're model-worthy. I work in the emergency room, where I'm fully clothed every day, most of the time in baggy scrubs. I do not have the body to be modeling underwear."

He scowls at me. "Yeah, you do."

"No." I shake my head. Panic has me in its grip.

"Come on. I've seen you in a swimsuit. It's practically the

same thing."

"I saw those briefs. They aren't boxers like a swimsuit, they're tight and clingy and they're going to show parts of you I haven't seen before." Unless you count the one or two times I've walked in on Cooper. Even then, I never saw his full package. I've imagined it, but... ugh... I need to clear my mind of this damn image.

There's a knock on the door before the woman calls, "Ready?"

"Sure, now she sounds all sweet," I grumble.

Cooper opens the door. "Let's just get this over with and then you can start planning that vacation."

I close my eyes. Beach, water, waves, sand, a good book. No alarms, bells, or patients being disorderly.

I open my eyes. It's the same as a swimsuit. Cooper is right. "Okay, let's go."

"That's my girl," Cooper says.

I love it when he calls me his girl, but right now, it sounds more like a father saying it to his daughter than anything romantic.

We walk onto the set, and I see that Bradley has scored himself a chair. How did I forget about him being here? He's got chips and a slice of pizza on a plate on his lap now.

My shin hits something soft, and I look down to see that I ran into a bed. A bed that wasn't here earlier. Panic erupts through me again. They deal with Cooper first, and he undoes his robe as if he doesn't have a care in the world. And why would he? He's like a bloody god. I can't even tell you the last time I lifted weights—unless helping a nurse get a three-hundred-pound man back into his bed counts.

I've seen Cooper almost naked before, but it's been a while. I soak up the image of his abs as they dip and crest along his stomach. The little patch of hair from his belly button disappears down past the elastic waist of the black briefs, where his package looks all snug and perfect. God, I turn my head and discreetly wipe my mouth in case I'm drooling.

"Now you. Take off the robe and slide in right under that white sheet next to Cooper," the woman says.

Cooper is about to laugh. I can see it in his eyes. He knows how freaked out I am about this, but he also knows I'll do it because I'd do just about anything for him.

He pulls the sheet back beside him. "Come on, sweetie."

I roll my eyes and untie my robe. It drops to the floor, and I dive under the covers before anyone else gets a good view—I hope.

"We've shared a bed before," Cooper says, as though that's going to put me at ease.

"Not in our underwear and not with twenty sets of eyes on us."

Once Cooper is in the position they want on top of the blanket, the photographer comes closer and snaps pictures while giving us directions. I'm sitting up with the bra showing in one picture, and in another one, I have a bare leg out and just part of my underwear showing. He gets Cooper to lie across the bed and rest his head on my stomach. We pretend to read a book, my head on his shoulder, his ankles crossed. His cologne smells good, and his skin is way softer than I would have imagined.

Jesus. What is this? I haven't felt this kind of need for Cooper in a long time.

"Can we try something different now that you guys are more comfortable?" The photographer studies us as though he's thinking.

"Of course," we say in unison.

"Cooper, put your back against the headboard. Ellery, straddle him."

"What?" My mouth drops open.

"It'll probably be used for international print, but while I have you both, I'd like to take it and see how it turns out."

"Beach," Cooper whispers in my ear.

He sits back, and I lift one leg and straddle him. My tits are at his eye level, and he stares at them for a moment before licking his lips.

"Coop!" I whisper-shout.

He shrugs. "I'm a man, Elle."

"I'm your best friend."

He turns his head so he can speak directly in my ear and no one will hear. "You're also a man's wet dream. I mean, you're spilling out of this damn thing. Your nipple is centimeters from my mouth, and your pussy is sitting on top of my dick. Prepare for a little surprise down there shortly."

I blink rapidly, shocked by the words coming out of his mouth. He's saying them so matter-of-factly that I'm not sure what to make of it. It's not as if he's coming on to me, but he doesn't usually speak to me like this.

Moments later, sure enough, he's hard underneath me. And from the look on his face, he's not even ashamed of it.

Part of me likes that his body has this reaction to me, that I'm not so friend-zoned that I can't arouse him, but still, we're doing a photo shoot.

"It's a natural reaction, Elle. I'm pretty sure you're wet down there, and if you aren't, just shoot me now."

I press my lips together to keep from saying something stupid that I'll regret. Because I am wet, especially the harder he becomes. And he's right. It is a natural reaction, and it doesn't have anything to do with the fact that it's him and me. He would know since he's done other shoots with female models. Though the idea of him getting hard over them makes me frown.

"Maybe look a little happier to be in bed with him," the photographer says, and I right my expression.

We finish the shoot, and I grab my robe and head right to my dressing room, thankful it's over. Maybe those feelings for Cooper haven't disappeared like I thought they did.

CHAPTER 8

COOPER

"Thanks for letting me get ready here," Ellery says from my bedroom. "I can't believe my next door neighbor blew all the fuses because he's trying to run a restaurant out of his apartment. My landlord said he'll have it all fixed by tonight."

"No problem." I stare into the mirror in my bathroom, attempting again to tie the bowtie for my tuxedo.

She comes in wearing her robe, her hair and makeup already done. She stops and laughs when she sees me. "What would you do without me?"

I let go of the ends in frustration, and she weaves between me and the counter, sits up on it, and takes the ends in her hands.

"I'd have asked Damon. He's a master at them."

Her smile dips for a second. "Well, since I've always been your bowtie girl, I'm glad I'm here."

Our eyes meet, and she quickly looks away. Elle's been tying them for me as long as we've been friends.

"It is convenient."

She hums to herself as she ties the tie and undoes it to do

it over again. Her perfectionism shines through. "I'm nervous about tonight."

"Why?" I try not to stare at her mouth, or her. Rather, I look over her shoulder in the mirror.

"My speech. I mean, you know how much this means to my dad. To expand our level of care, especially in the ER, is huge."

"You're going to do great. Just like you always do when you speak in front of people. I'm the one who freezes up." We both laugh, knowing it's the truth.

"Well, if I can give my speech as well as I can tie this bowtie, then I'll do awesome. You look very dashing, Mr. Rice." She hops off the counter.

My hands itch to grab her hips and put her back up on the edge. To spread her legs open and step into the space between them. Untie the robe and let it fall open, exposing her.

But she's not mine, and she's already halfway to my room. "I better get in my dress."

The buzzer rings from the security gate downstairs.

"Oh, that's probably Bradley. Let him up?" She smiles and shuts the bedroom door.

I head over to the intercom. "Yeah?" I answer.

"Hey, Coop, it's Bradley," he says.

Jaw clenched, I click the buzzer, hoping maybe he's not fast enough, but the knock on my door a minute later says he was.

"Come in," I say, heading for my jacket hanging in the closet.

"Hey." He walks in wearing a black-and-turquoise-flowered tuxedo. He'll definitely stand out. I wonder what Mr. Wallace will think of this.

"Nice tux," I say, raising my eyebrows.

He puffs out his chest and smooths his hands down his front. "I like to be different." He stares at my typical black-and-white tux.

"It's a classic look, yes." I shrug on my coat. "She'll be out in a minute. Drink?"

"Sure."

I go to my fridge and open a beer, passing it to him before opening mine.

"So, anything I should know for tonight?" he asks. "Ellery said she usually takes you."

"Well, I buy a table every year to support the hospital. This year, the push is to expand the services in the ER. There'll be a private auction too." It's a gentle nudge for him to do something. Bradley doesn't make the kind of money I do, but he makes enough to buy something at the private auction.

"Oh, a table. And we're sitting…"

"At my table."

He nods.

My bedroom door opens, and I'm thankful because, since Bradley started dating Ellery, I don't have much to talk to him about. I'm not even interested in being around him most of the time.

Ellery walks out of the room wearing a silver dress that molds along her hips, fitting her perfectly. The fabric dips at her breasts but doesn't give away her cleavage. Her heels make her even taller than she already is, but Bradley and I have inches on her still.

"You're stunning," Bradley says, taking the words out of my mouth.

I can't stop my gaze from soaking her in. Her hair is swept to one side, a little wavy, exposing her neck. She's so damn beautiful it makes my chest ache.

"Thank you, you look very handsome," she says, approaching Bradley, then straightening his bowtie. "Love this tuxedo. So different."

I feel like a parent watching their kids at prom. Strike that, because I'm pretty sure my dad wasn't lusting after my prom date like I am Ellery in this moment.

"Thanks. I think Coop doesn't like it." He smiles at me.

Elle gives me the once-over and smiles. "He's just the more traditional type. Let's go get the others and head out."

I pocket my keys and wallet, waiting for them to go first.

We meet Miles, Bryce, Damon, and Adeline at the bottom of the stairs by the limo we rented. The girls are gushing over how good they all look, while Damon and Miles give Bradley hell about his suit. Although Damon's is magenta velvet, so I don't know why he's giving anyone grief.

I speak to the driver and give him the address of where we need to stop on the way to the event, and he nods.

There's alcohol and champagne in the back of the limo, and Bradley is the first to help himself to it. I sit back, happy to have gotten a spot by the door.

Soon, the limo slows, and everyone looks around.

"I'll be right back," I say, filing out.

"Why are we stopping? I can't be late, Coop," Ellery says.

I peek my head back in. "I'm just picking up Maya."

"Maya?" She blinks in surprise.

I turn on the walkway of the four-flat apartment building and make my way over to the building.

I didn't mention to Ellery that I was bringing Maya because I didn't decide until the last minute. And then I wasn't sure how to tell Ellery, though I don't know why it feels awkward. She has her own date for tonight.

Maya opens her door before I reach the stairs, and she comes out.

I met Maya at the grocery store, where we kept running into one another in the aisles and then at checkout. She lifted a magazine and saw my ad on the back cover, then looked at me. She said she didn't know who I was, and I'm a sucker for that, so I asked her to meet me after the game the other day. We haven't officially dated, but I needed a date tonight, so I asked her. I'm not sure it's heading anywhere though.

She's wearing a red dress that shows off her cute figure. As much as I wish the closed-throat feeling would wash over me like it did with Ellery moments ago, it doesn't. I'm fully capable of taking a full breath.

She walks down the stairs in her heels like a pro, and I offer her my arm.

"You look beautiful," I say.

"You look good too. I'm so nervous." She bites her bottom lip.

"Don't be. You've already met my friends."

I open the car door for her and have her file into the limo first. As I climb in after her, all my friends say hello, and the girls compliment her dress.

So far, so good.

We arrive at the venue holding the event. The hospital did an amazing job with the decorations, and we get our pictures taken on the red carpet. Once inside, we scope out where we're going to sit. Bryce and Miles are acting weird and disappear shortly after they grab their table assignment.

"I don't want to know," I say.

"Let's remember they have history at these kinds of events," Ellery says, and I remember the story of how they first got together back in San Francisco.

I'm about to head to the bar with Maya when I hear my name called across the room. I turn to see Ellery's mom coming our way.

"You look handsome as always." She places her hand on my cheek and smiles at me.

"Hi, Mrs. Wallace," I say, hugging her. "You look gorgeous yourself."

"Well, it takes a lot longer than it used to to look like this." She looks at Maya, and her smile diminishes a bit. "And who do we have here?"

I place my hand on the small of Maya's back. "This is my date, Maya."

She puts her hand out, and they shake, but Mrs. Wallace isn't nearly as welcoming as she usually is. Of course, usually her daughter is my date.

"Where is my daughter anyway?" Mrs. Wallace asks.

I gesture in Elle's direction. "She's that way with her date," I say pointedly.

Mrs. Wallace makes a sound in the back of her throat and heads off to see her daughter.

"That's Ellery's mom. Want that drink now?"

"Yes, please," Maya says.

We head to the bar, and she orders a wine while I get a mixed drink. Then we stand around, waiting for things to start.

"So, this is for Mercy Hospital?" Maya asks.

A video plays on a giant screen at the front of the room. Ellery shows up on every fifth slide, helping someone in emergency care.

"Yeah. They want to expand their emergency room. Ellery is a doctor there. She'll be giving a speech about it later."

"Oh, nice." She shifts on her feet and glances around.

"Are you okay?"

She nods. "Yeah, it's just that in the limo, I felt a little uncomfortable. I'm not sure your friends like me."

"Well, I do, and that's all that matters," I say, pulling her closer to me, willing myself to be interested in this beautiful woman.

I probably should have prepared everyone by telling them that Maya was joining us, so that's on me. But damn them for being weird around her when they've accepted Bradley with open fucking arms.

A little while later, we're told to take a seat, so I lead us over to our table. We sit with Miles on my left and Bradley on Maya's right.

Mr. Wallace goes up first to speak to the crowd and thank everyone.

"That's Ellery's dad," I whisper to Maya, my arm around the back of her chair.

Ellery looks over her shoulder, hearing me, but turns back to face the front of the room.

"And now may I present to you, my daughter. She's going to pull on those heartstrings and magically get you to open up those pocketbooks of yours. She's done it my entire life, so I'm warning you now."

The whole room laughs.

Ellery winds through the tables, and people she knows reach out to her to say a quick hello. By the time she reaches the stage, I'm exhausted for her.

"Good evening, everyone. My father isn't wrong, I'm going to try to use my charm to divest you of some money tonight."

The room laughs.

Mr. Wallace puts his arm around her and pulls her to him, kissing her temple. Although Mr. Wallace is definitely bossy like my father was, I've always admired their relationship. You can see how proud he is of her.

She continues her speech, getting the laughs right when she wants them. The room quiets when she discusses how many patients they've had to re-route ambulances for because they were at capacity and how no doctor goes into medicine to not be able to help those who need care. She speaks about how emergencies are a critical time where intervention can change an outcome and how sending patients to a different hospital isn't ideal. Everyone claps when she ends her speech by saying that every dollar counts and asking people to think about bidding on the silent auction.

Ellery's eyes search out mine on her way back, and I smile and nod to let her know she did a great job. The music starts before she's made it back to our table, and some couples head out to the dance floor. I'm so transfixed by Elle that I don't notice Bradley meeting her halfway across the room. I watch as he links his fingers with hers and escorts her onto the dance floor. She's usually against dancing at this event, always saying that she needs to schmooze everyone.

He holds her close, and her head is in the crook of his neck, their intertwined hands tucked into their bodies as he parades her around as if they're on the *Dancing with the Stars* television show. That punch of red-hot jealousy hits me, but I can't strip my eyes off them.

"I'm gonna go to the bathroom," Maya says, but I don't respond.

My feelings for Ellery are ramping up, not diminishing the longer she's with him. My gaze shoots to Maya's backside as she leaves the room. She's sweet and adorable. I should want her, but no matter what, it's always been Elle for me.

It's unfair to Maya for me to continue things with her when I feel this way. I'll have to tell her tonight that there's no future for us.

I slide my chair out to go over and ask to step in on their dance, but Dr. Wallace steps in before I can.

Fuck.

It's probably better that way anyway. Ellery is the one who made me promise her never to cross that line after that fateful night in college.

CHAPTER 9

ELLERY

I'm mid-shift on Saturday when Jennifer from the intake desk calls back. I happen to be looking up something about a patient, so I answer the phone.

"Hey, Dr. Wallace, sorry to bother you, but a package was just delivered for you."

"Oh okay. I'll be out to get it in a second."

"Thanks. If I get a chance, I'll walk it back, but Olivia called in sick, so I'm by myself."

"It's honestly no problem."

I leave my computer and head out to the intake desk. It's a big box, and I'm worried about what it could be. "Thanks, Jennifer."

"Let me know what Cooper sent you!" She's smiling wide.

Cooper has fans everywhere.

"I'll let you know, but I'm not sure why he'd send me anything."

I head into the back. It's not unheard of for me to get things from Cooper. In fact, he sends things to the whole department all the time. Food mostly, especially on holidays.

A mystery box though? I'm stumped.

Things have been kind of weird between us lately. Maybe this is Cooper's way of clearing the air.

Alice and Hayes walk over, arguing about something, and stop to watch me open the box.

"Jeez, Cooper makes every other boyfriend look horrible," Hayes says.

"He's my best friend, not my boyfriend." I slide my fingernail across the tape on the top of the box.

"Exactly. The fact that someone's best friend does all this, what does that say about boyfriends?" Hayes rolls his eyes and wheels his chair over to one of the computers. "And now I'm going to school Alice and prove her wrong."

"No, you aren't." Alice looks at the box, then at me. She gestures excitedly with her hands. "Open it."

I open the box to find a dark blue Grizzlies jersey, but it's not Cooper's number. I lift it out of the box, and a notecard falls to the floor. I think my stomach falls to the floor with it.

"That's not Cooper's number," Hayes says. "Man, are things getting serious with the new guy?"

"What the hell? I'm offended for Cooper." Alice picks up the notecard before handing it to me.

"This Bradley guy knows he's got big shoes to fill. I mean, we've come to expect things from the man in your life," Hayes says.

I stare at both of them for a beat before opening the notecard.

"Oh, look. Another glimpse into Dr. Wallace's love life. Do let me sit here and gawk over the gossip." Dr. Murphy leans on the desk, placing his chin in his palm and staring at all of us with a creepy smile.

"We just wanted to see what was in the package." Alice smiles.

"Hey, I'm researching something on the computer actually." Hayes buries his head back in the computer.

"All my patients are taken care of," I tell Dr. Murphy, leaning back in the chair and opening the notecard.

> *Ellery,*
>
> *I'd love to show everyone that you're my girl. You'll find my jersey and some stickers with my number to put on your cheeks. I hope I'm not stepping too far over the line. I'll see you up in the stands wearing my jersey tomorrow.*
>
> *Bradley*

I stuff the card back in the envelope. I can't do this. I mean, I've been wearing Cooper's number forever. My mind floats back to the very first game I wore it and how what was originally a joke turned into a ritual. Back when I thought there was still a chance for us to be something more.

We were still in our junior year, and Cooper was still pushing me to date him. I was unsure. What his dad had said made a lot of sense. Cooper had a football career to fulfill, and I wasn't going to get into medical school if I kept spending all my time with him. Putting off our career goals in the name of something that could be fleeting felt shortsighted.

We'd often go to the coffee shop where we'd say we were going to study but ended up people watching out a window. Cooper would do these little voices like he was narrating the conversations we couldn't hear. He even had voices for dogs.

He had this way of bringing me out of myself, out of my head. He made me smile. Made me not take everything so seriously. It made me eager to see him when we weren't together. I was falling for him, and it scared me because I'd never liked anyone as much as him.

We were sitting in the coffee shop when a girl walked by wearing his jersey. It was oversized and might have been her boyfriend's, but it made me wonder.

"Do you like the fact so many people wear your number?" I sipped my coffee, looking at him.

"I don't really care. A lot of girls do it because they want my attention."

"The girls on this campus definitely want your attention. Have you seen the sneers I get? There was one girl at the student center the other day who asked if we were dating. She was near tears, and her friend just looked at me. I felt bad for her. Except when I told her no, her eyes got that dreamy look in them. One day you'll find a girl in your bed, uninvited. Some stalker."

He laughed. "Then do me a favor and wear my jersey and paint my number on your cheek tomorrow?"

"No, I'll get jumped." I laughed.

"You wouldn't be the only one, but you are the only one I give the good tickets to."

"I'm probably the only one of them who watches the game." I leaned back in my seat.

The next morning after my lab, I rushed home to get ready to go to Cooper's game. When football games started taking precedence over everything else in my life, I didn't know. His dad was right—our lives were weaving together, and we were just friends. What would happen if we brought sex and love into it? I couldn't imagine not wanting Cooper every second of every day. So being just friends definitely made more sense, even if Cooper made it really hard.

"Something came for you. I put it on your bed," Bryce hollered to me from the bathroom.

"Thanks."

I went into my bedroom, and sure enough, there was a box on my bed. It didn't have a shipping label on it.

"What is it?" Bryce peeked her head in, her toothbrush hanging out of her mouth.

"I haven't opened it. Who dropped it off?"

She shrugged. "Some freshman football player."

"So it's from Cooper?" I sat on the bed and dug through tissue paper. I laughed when I pulled out the jersey and held it up to Bryce. "It's his jersey."

Her eyes widened, and she bit her lip. "Mark my words—you guys will have sex before the end of the semester." She walked back to the bathroom.

"It's just a joke. Because of all the girls who wear his jersey. He thinks if I do, some of them will lay off. But I don't think so." I couldn't say it wasn't tempting though. To be known as Cooper Rice's girlfriend wouldn't be the worst thing in the world.

"You're doing it!" Bryce shouted from down the hall.

I held the shirt up in front of me. I really wanted to wear it, joke or not.

So that day, when Cooper came out of the tunnel and looked up at me, I had on the jersey, his number painted on both cheeks, and my hair pulled back. Our eyes found each other and locked. This little thing sprouted in my stomach, taking life, because what I saw in his eyes wasn't anything I'd seen before.

When he got drafted, he sent me his jersey for his new team, and it'd been like that for as long as I could remember.

I stare at Bradley's jersey, wondering how on Earth I can show up with it on. Luckily, I'm called into a room. I shove the box in the cabinet below, pushing off that decision for a later time.

Bryce and Adeline are already seated at the fifty-yard line, both of them wearing their husbands' jerseys. Bryce has taken it to a whole new level with earrings, clips for her hair, and necklaces. Everything has Miles's number on it. Adeline is alone, so she must have opted not to bring Clover today.

I have my beer and popcorn, my must-haves for a game. As I slide through the row, Adeline and Bryce look up to see me coming.

"What the hell?" Bryce says.

Adeline doesn't say anything, but her mouth is hanging open.

"What are you wearing?" Bryce whispers when I get closer.

"Just stop." I look around, the feeling of betrayal hitting me from every direction. But I'm not dating Cooper, I'm dating Bradley, and he deserves to know I support him. If the roles were reversed and Bradley was wearing some other girl's number, I'm sure these two would have something to say about that.

"Okay." Bryce mimes zipping her lips shut.

Adeline looks over and pats my leg. She really has that whole mom thing down. "I get it. And I'm sure Cooper will understand.'

"Oh no." Bryce shakes her head. "He will *not* understand. I mean, you needed one of those half-and-half jerseys made. Don't be surprised if Cooper climbs up here and tears it off your body."

I roll my eyes. "You're so dramatic."

She turns toward me. "Do you even like Bradley this much?" She runs her hand down my arm.

"Hello, you're my friend. You're supposed to have my back."

Her face softens, and she opens her mouth but shuts it. "You're right, but I can't help but hurt for Cooper. He's my friend too."

I swallow the guilt that's threatening to suffocate me.

"Guys," Adeline says, but what else is she going to say? She doesn't know the entire story. No one does. Bryce is our closest friend, and I think she's becoming as confused as I am. "Here they come! I hope Damon's not upset, but Clover is breaking a tooth, and she's not very cooperative. She would not have made a good cheerleader today."

"He'll be excited to have you to himself for a night. I'm assuming Miles and I are by ourselves after the game?" Bryce sips her beer. "Because Cooper is going to disappear, and you'll be busy with Bradley."

"We'll go out," Adeline says, but then Damon comes to the wall like he does before every home game.

"Alone tonight?" He waggles his eyebrows.

Adeline laughs and bends down to kiss him. "She's at my parents'."

He bites his lip and stares at her as though he could take her right here and now. God, what it must feel like to be wanted by a man like that.

"We're going out after the game," Adeline says.

He kisses her quickly on the lips.

"Siska! I'm going to bench you!" Coach Stone yells like he does every home game.

"No, we're not." Damon winks at Adeline, then moves to jump down off the ledge but stops when he notices what I'm wearing. His eyebrows raise, and his mouth hangs open. "Oh shit."

As he lands on the ground, I blow out a breath. I look at the field and see Bradley looking at me with such a big smile that, for a second, I'm glad I did it. Then I glance behind him. Cooper stands there, his hands nestled in the warmer at his waist. He doesn't show any reaction but turns away and goes to talk to one of the coaches.

"Ugh, I need another beer," Bryce says. "This takes me back to childhood when Mommy and Daddy would fight."

"Grow up, Bryce," I say. "I had no choice."

"That's where you're wrong. You always have a choice. And I don't blame you. If I were you and Miles were Coop, I would've pulled this shit a long time ago. At some point in the very near future, one of you is going to have to admit your feelings to the other before you keep bringing innocent people who will only get hurt into the mix."

"I'm not pulling any shit." I stand. "I have to go to the bathroom."

"Want me to come?" Adeline asks.

"No," I say sharply, then feeling bad, I turn around. "Thank you though."

I hear Adeline talking to Bryce about calming down, and Bryce tells her she's been dealing with this crap for almost ten years.

I don't know, maybe Bryce is right.

When I reach the bathroom, I pretend to go and wash my hands, then I move to an empty station without a sink to check my makeup.

At this point, our friendship isn't going to hold up. It's inevitable we'll meet other people who mean something to us someday, and we're doing a terrible job of navigating that change. Things are going to come between us. Just like this stupid jersey. I stare at Bradley's number and feel sick to my stomach.

And if that's the case, what was the point of us not crossing the line so we wouldn't ruin our friendship?

CHAPTER 10
COOPER

I'm thankful for an away game this week so that I don't have to look up in the stands and see Ellery in his jersey. I don't have to see Ellery and Bradley get into the same car after the game. I don't have to be the seventh wheel with all my friends.

"Wait, they asked Ellery to model?" Damon holds up his hand on the plane.

Damon just got around to asking me how things went with my latest endorsement deal, so I'm filling him in. Thankfully, Bradley is all the way in the back.

"Yeah, we were in our underwear. Most of the time she was under the sheet, but we have a few shots where she wasn't." I've been on the fence about coming clean to my friends about what the whole experience was like. It's not like it changes anything. I've dealt with these feelings for Elle on and off through the years.

They'll disappear soon.

Once she and Bradley don't work out.

"Was that the first time?" Miles asks.

"The first time I've seen her in her underwear? No, I've

seen her naked. By accident, when we were getting massages once," I rush to add.

Her body hasn't changed since then. She might not work out, but the steps she walks in the emergency room are enough to keep her fit. I had to hurry and put on my robe after we were done to hide my erection from everyone else.

"Why do I miss all the fun times?" Damon asks.

Miles doesn't say anything. I haven't known him as long as I have Damon, but he's definitely the one of the three of us who is most invested in his friends' happiness. I've thought about talking to him only, but Damon would feel betrayed, and in reality, Damon's outlook on life has changed since he got with Adeline and became a father.

"I know I've only known you a few years, but you and Ellery, why haven't you ever…" Miles asks.

I glance behind me. Since we're flying during the day, no one is sleeping, so it's loud and hard to listen in on conversations.

"Because they're blind," Damon says. "And stubborn as hell."

I sip my drink and straighten in my seat. "It's more about the fact that I can't lose her. And let's face it, relationships come and go. Sure, we can say that if it didn't work out, we could go back to being friends. But we've been through so much together, I can't imagine what it would be like one day if that was over."

"I can see that. But let me play devil's advocate with you," Miles says.

I nod.

"Since she's been with Bradley, your time with her has been limited, right?"

I nod again.

"So, eventually one of you is going to meet and marry someone else and your time with her will be even more limited. Plus, I don't know a lot of women who are okay with their boyfriend having a best friend who is a girl and spending so much time with her."

He and Damon nod in unison as if it were choreographed.

"Then she's not the one for me." I shrug. "And if I met someone, she would never take me away from Ellery."

I get where Miles is coming from. I've had the same thoughts over the years. The older we get, the better the chances are of one of us meeting someone serious and our friendship becoming strained. I hope it's not Bradley, but she's spent a lot of time with him lately. And she's always smiling and laughing, so I assume she really likes him. I can't stomach asking her about it.

The pilot gets on the intercom and announces that we're starting our descent.

"I hope it turns out for you," Miles says.

"Even if you're being delusional about the whole thing. The only way to keep her in your life is to admit you want her and take the plunge." Damon chimes in with his two cents.

"I'm not delusional. Haven't you ever worried about losing someone?" I ask.

"Do you have any idea how horrible it could've been for me if Adeline and I hadn't turned out the way we have? She would've been a part of my life, no matter what, for the rest of my life. We share a child. But I took the chance. And it paid off—big time." He grins.

The difference is that we're completely different people, and they have no idea what Ellery and I have been through together. Damon and Adeline have never almost lost the other one for good.

The plane lands on the runway, and I'm thankful to end this conversation. Neither of them understands what's at stake if I lose my friendship with Ellery.

We win the game against the Kingsmen, and since fog has descended on the area, we're stuck in San Francisco until morning. Usually, I only go out with the team a couple of times in a season, but since Miles used to play for the Kingsmen and still has friends on the team, I decided to join them.

We're at the hotel bar, having a drink while we wait for the cars we ordered. Looks like a lot of the single guys are going out tonight. We're at the part of the season where everyone needs to blow off some steam.

"Lee, Brady, and Chase are all meeting us at the club. Already reserved a few VIP sections." Miles shoves his phone into his pocket.

I tip my beer to my lips. "Sounds good."

Bradley hangs out farther down the bar with a few of the newer guys. He appears to be the loudest one between them, which doesn't surprise me. I've wondered why Ellery likes him because she was attracted to me at one time too, and we're very different. I'm more reserved, keeping to myself while Bradley makes sure everyone knows he's in the room.

I've got to shake this comparison game I've got going on in my head. It's not like I've made myself available to Ellery after that night. Nothing scared me more.

Someone comes in and tells us our rides are here, so we all tally the bills and file out to the cars. As usual, I'm with Damon and Miles.

The club has a long line outside—probably because it's a Thursday night. I hate the weekday games, but at least I've got Sunday off this week.

We get out, and the doormen surround us, allowing us in while people either call our names or say we suck ass since we beat their team. The three Kingsmen are already in the VIP section, drinking around a round table.

"You look like a bunch of old men," Miles says, yawning.

"Talk to your nephew," Chase says.

It's obvious to me that Chase doesn't really want to be here, but he's marrying Miles's sister. I'm not sure this is his scene.

"And I owe Twyla…" Miles cuts him a look, and Chase chuckles. "I'll keep it to myself. But I'm indebted to her for letting me go out tonight, even if I'd rather be anywhere else than at a club."

"None of your wives came?" Damon asks.

"Please, your ass wouldn't even be here if they played in Chicago," I say.

"I did enough partying before Adeline that it's out of my system." He smiles and waves over the waitress with that usual charm of his.

She's all smiles, looking over each one of us. "What can I get you?"

We all order our drinks, and the space slowly fills in with our players.

"Helluva game today," Lee says. "Think you're gonna get three rings?"

I shake my head. "I have a lot of players I owe it to if I do. It's not just me."

He nods. Being a quarterback himself, he understands.

A few girls are allowed in the VIP area, sauntering by our table, and I realize I'm the only single one in our group.

"All yours," Brady Banks says with a chuckle.

"Didn't Miles tell me you first met Violet here?" Damon asks.

Lee and Chase both laugh while Brady's face goes a little red. "Yeah, and she wanted nothing to do with me after she spent the night with me."

Now we're all laughing at his expense.

When the laughter dies down, the three Kingsmen look at me.

"You seeing someone?" Lee asks.

"His best friend, who happens to be dating Bradley on our

team." Damon lifts his eyebrows as if he's challenging me to deny it.

And because I'm an idiot, I stand, calling him on his bluff. Ellery is living her life. I can too.

I approach the first pretty blonde I see because I like blondes, and she instantly knows who I am. She says my name with a sultry, seductive tone, and her gaze floats down my body. I'm in a pair of jeans and a button-down shirt untucked.

"I'm Kyla."

I take my own perusal of her body. She's definitely hot in her champagne-colored microdress. Her blonde hair is slicked back into a long ponytail, and her face is covered in makeup. She's nothing like Ellery.

Jesus, stop the comparison game.

"Let's dance," she says, her small, soft hand taking mine and leading me onto the dance floor.

I glance over at the guys, and they all raise their drinks. Why do I feel as though I'm on the wrong side here? I'm usually in the booth, drinking a few before I can sneak out and take an Uber back to the hotel or home.

Kyla places my hands on her hips, and she rotates them, grinding into my crotch in a circular motion, tilting her head back to look at me while one arm wraps around my neck. She's expecting me to kiss her, but screw that.

Eventually, I do relax enough to get into the music, knowing if I'm ever going to get over Ellery, this is what I need to do—put myself out there. Kyla might not be looking to lock down a player. Maybe she's looking for a good time too. And her body does feel good on my hands. My dick stirs, and that's a good sign since she's hot as hell.

Soon, I'm controlling her hips.

"You like that?" she asks loudly enough for me to hear her over the pounding music. "Want to go to the bathroom?" She turns and wraps her arms around my neck. "Or you can take me back to your hotel room. I'll sign whatever NDA you want me to." Her hand runs down the front of my body, past the buttons on my shirt, and cups my dick.

Fuck. Why do I want to turn and run?

She lifts on her tiptoes, wanting a kiss, and I place my hand on the back of her neck, ready to do just that. My eyes close and her lips press to mine, but all I see behind my eyelids is Ellery. Her plump, soft lips that she's constantly putting lip balm on. Her body pressed against mine during that photo shoot. Not Kyla, some random woman out to score with me tonight.

I open my eyes and drop my hand, stepping back. "I'm sorry, I can't."

"Ohhh… you have someone. Well, your secret is safe with me. I don't really care about girlfriends or wives." She reaches for my crotch again, but I grab her wrist and hold her back.

"I do and…" My gaze snags on the image behind her of a big body hovering over a woman as his hands glide along her body. "Excuse me."

I breeze past Kyla and shove people out of the way until I pull Bradley off of the woman.

"What the fuck?" Bradley says, and the lipstick on the corner of his mouth tells me everything I need to know.

I push him in the chest. "What the fuck are you doing?"

"What does it look like I'm doing?" He seems as if he might be on his way to being drunk.

"You're dating Ellery!" I shout.

Before I know it, Damon and Miles are down by us, shoulder to shoulder with me.

"We're not in a committed relationship." Bradley takes the woman and wraps his arm around her waist.

"So what? This can't be happening if she's in your life." I motion to the woman.

He laughs. "Give me a fucking break. She hasn't even spread her legs or sucked my dick yet."

"Shit," I hear Damon say right before I cock my fist back and slam it into Bradley's face.

Fuck the consequences.

Bradley holds his face where I just hit him, eyes narrowed. "Jesus, I always knew you had a thing for her. That you never wanted me to date her." He shakes his head, widening his jaw, opening and shutting it.

"This has nothing to do with me and everything to do with the respect that you should have for her. She's an intelligent, caring, beautiful woman and you're throwing her aside for what? Some woman who only wants your dick so she can say she bagged a professional football player?"

"That's the problem, Cooper. Ellery doesn't seem to want my dick."

I burst forward to go after him, but Damon and Miles pull me back just as the bouncers show up.

"I'm gonna kill him," I say, fighting against their hold.

"Time to say good night, Coop," Damon says. "You aren't playing well with others."

Before I know it, we're in a taxi on the way back to the hotel.

Now I'm going to have to tell Ellery what happened, and I'm gonna hate seeing that look on her face.

CHAPTER 11

ELLERY

I read the text message again and take a seat on my couch.

> Bradley: I'm sure you've heard by now, but I'd really like you to hear my side.

Figuring I want to know exactly what he's talking about, I call Bryce before I respond. After the last home game, she apologized and reminded me how much she hates change.

She picks up on the first ring. "What's up, buttercup?"

"Well, someone's in a good mood this morning."

"Miles just got home."

"I thought they were supposed to be home last night?"

"Too much fog, so they stayed the night in San Francisco and took the early morning flight out."

All things I'd probably know if Cooper and I weren't in this weird space with our friendship. Hell, he probably would've come to my place, and we'd have gone to breakfast this morning. It makes me realize how much I miss us.

"Bradley sent me a cryptic message." I fiddle with my pajama pants.

"What did he say?" she asks in her same chipper mood. "Oh, wait. Miles has a look on his face."

Shit. I felt this buildup between Cooper and Bradley over the past few weeks, and now I think the powder keg blew.

"Shut up!" Bryce says to Miles.

"What?" I grip the phone tighter.

"No way he did that. Really, Miles?" she says.

"Miles what?"

"What a douche!" she says.

"Bryce, what is it?" I grow more and more desperate for answers the longer she ignores me.

"Way to go." She claps. "Oh. Well, that's…"

"Bryce!"

"Okay. Okay. Miles, you have to get off me so I can tell her."

A hefty groan echoes from behind her. "I'm taking a shower. Hurry up and join me," he says loudly enough for me to hear.

Can't say I'm not jealous.

"What is it?" I ask again with a pleading note in my voice.

"I guess they all went out last night."

"Cooper too?" He doesn't usually party after games.

"Well, I think this whole Bradley thing has him off-kilter." She sighs. "I guess Cooper was on the dance floor with a woman."

Nausea rumbles in my stomach.

"But so was Bradley," she says hesitantly as if it's going to crush me.

"Yeah?"

"Cooper lost it, words were exchanged, and Cooper punched Bradley before Miles and Damon got him out of there. As of right now, I haven't heard anything about it, but… it's early in San Francisco. All those pictures and videos are sitting on people's phones waiting to circulate if they aren't already."

"Is this going to hurt Cooper's career?" It's my first thought.

"That's all you care about? How about Bradley dancing with someone else? I hate telling you this, but Miles said he had the impression it wouldn't have ended with dancing."

"We're not exclusive."

"Are you seeing other people?" she asks.

She knows the answer. I don't do random hookups. Wouldn't have the time to even if I wanted to.

"You know I'm not."

"Well then…"

"Cooper shouldn't have done what he did. He's just gone and made it a bigger deal than it needed to be. It's none of his business."

"Elle," she says with that tone I hate so much because it usually means she's about to throw some truth my way. "We both know you've been Cooper's business since junior year of college."

"Come on!" Miles shouts in the background.

"Go. We'll talk later." I stand, unable to sit anymore with all this nervous energy rolling through me.

"No, Miles can wait. Want to meet up for lunch or something?"

She really is a great friend.

"No, spend the day with Miles. Just let me know when you see anything in the media. I want to be prepared for when my dad and everyone else sees it."

"Done, and I'll try to squash as much as I can on my end, but we're just one publication."

"Thanks."

"It'll all blow over, Elle." Bryce covers the phone. "Miles, you act like we haven't had sex in a week when you had me bent over the couch before you left for San Francisco," she shouts.

"Go," I insist.

"Love you," she says.

"Love you back."

We hang up, and I pace my living room, pulling up Bradley's text message. I could call Cooper and get his side of it. Him playing protector pisses me off, especially since I'm not sure if he did it for my benefit or his. Bradley and I aren't close to being exclusive—I haven't even slept with the man.

I hammer out a message before I become a chickenshit.

> Me: Breakfast?

Bradley: Name the time and place, and I'm there.

> Me: In an hour at Gloria's on Lincoln.

Bradley: See you then.

I set my phone on the coffee table and head into the shower, thankful this is my day off. If this fight goes public and, for some reason, my name gets mentioned, I do not want to face Dr. Murphy and his snide remarks.

The worst part is that Cooper has yet to reach out to me. I should've been his first call, which tells me a lot about the state of our friendship.

I miss him so much. Is this what we're in for when one of us gets into a serious relationship? It's going to change us, and I'm not prepared for that, as much as I guess I need to be.

Bradley's already sitting at a table by the window when I arrive. He's talking to the waitress when the hostess shows me over, his black eye on display. They're talking about how the game went yesterday, and I inwardly roll my eyes. Cooper would've been in the back of the restaurant with a hat and sunglasses on so no one would recognize him. But I have to stop comparing every man to Cooper.

Bradley stands when I approach, waiting for me to take my seat before sitting back down. He's always had all the right moves, but now I'm wondering if those moves clouded my judgment. Maybe they aren't as genuine as I'd like to believe.

"Hi," he says, lifting the coffee carafe on the table.

I flip over the cup. "Please."

He pours me a cup, and I don't drink from it right away, letting it cool.

"I'm assuming Cooper has called you." He frowns.

"Actually, no, so I'm a little in the dark here."

He leans back, looking defeated. Clearly, he was hoping I already knew what went down, and then he could just explain his side—who the woman was and why he was with her. Although I'm not sure he owes me an explanation.

"Oh, I figured he would have."

I shake my head, pretending to be in the dark.

"Well… the fog in San Francisco was so bad, the plane couldn't get out, so a few of us went to a club. Surprisingly, Cooper went along with Damon and Miles. Probably cause of the Kingsmen." He shrugs.

I stare blankly at him, not caring about the whys or who else went out.

He clears his throat, obviously noticing my mood. "Anyway, we had some VIP areas, and I was on the dance floor with a woman. You know how they never really understand 'no.' I thought one dance would be okay. The next thing I know, Cooper stomps over and pushes me away from her. We exchanged words, and he punched me."

It's a similar story to Miles's, so at least he's kind of telling me the truth. But it's clear to me I'm not getting the whole story.

"What words were exchanged?"

"I just told him we weren't exclusive." He looks at his coffee mug, then out the window.

"And?"

"Listen, I might have had a little too much to drink, and when he came at me, I was pissed. He made this huge scene in the middle of the dance floor."

"What did you say, Bradley?" I bite my lip, not sure I want to know.

"I told him how we weren't having sex and that you… didn't want my dick."

I sink back in my chair. I'm sure that set Cooper off.

He leans over the table, reaching for me. "Ellery, I never meant to hurt you, but we're not exclusive, right? We've only been on a few dates, and yeah, I really like you, I just…"

I smile at him. Yeah, it's about time I admit the truth to myself. "You're right, we aren't in a committed relationship, but there's a big difference between us. One is that if I'm dating someone, I don't do hookups with other people. And I kind of want the person I'm dating to be the same way. Just because they want to put all their effort in with me." He opens his mouth to speak, and I raise my hand. "But I agree, we weren't exclusive, and if you'd hooked up with that girl, it wouldn't be like you were cheating—if that's what you want to be assured of. Regardless, I think we both know we might be trying to force something that just isn't here between us."

He chuckles and sips his coffee. "Forcing something? I think when you told me you were single, that was the first mistake."

I frown. "What do you mean?"

"You and Cooper. Give me a break. Everyone sees it. I was blind to it for a little while, believing the whole best friend act, but come on, you're both delusional if you don't admit you love one another."

I blink a couple of times. "We do love one another, but not like lovers."

He leans in close. "Have the two of you ever fucked?"

"Jesus." I narrow my eyes.

"I'm pretty sure you'd rather be with him than me. Just ask anyone at that photo shoot," he grumbles.

"What?" I stop myself from saying more, thinking that this is only going to get nastier the longer I sit here. "Listen, it's fine, but I think we're done here. I'll talk to Cooper because he shouldn't have punched you. I'm sure we'll run into one another at the games and events, and I'd like us to be able to be cordial with one another."

He agrees, and as I ready myself to leave, he stands and meets me at the edge of the table.

"Thanks, Ellery. I do wish it would've worked out." He hugs me.

"Take care, Bradley."

I walk out of the restaurant, my stomach rumbling with hunger, and grab another Uber. I have one last place to visit before I can bury my head under the covers for the rest of the day.

When I'm in the Uber, my phone dings with a message from Bryce.

> Bryce: This video shows the fight. I haven't seen that face on Cooper since he saw Jase Neighton leading you upstairs when you were drunk at that party in college.

. . .

I play the video. It's hard to hear the words between them, but Cooper punches Bradley, causing him to stumble back.

Another text from Bryce comes in.

> Bryce: This is the drunk girl Bradley was dancing with.

The girl is barely able to stand up as she tells her friends what happened while someone films her. "I was dancing with Bradley when Cooper Rice just came over and shoved him off me. Then they started fighting. At first, I thought it was about me, but I guess not. Cooper punched Bradley, and then they started yelling at each other. Damn, I thought I was gonna get lucky with a pro football player."

She pretends to pout, and my irritation gets worse.

> Me: Thanks. I just broke up with Bradley. Or stopped seeing him, I guess.

> Bryce: Good for you. Although these videos aren't good for Cooper, thankfully, no one is putting your name in there. But the people who know you guys will know it's about you. Just preparing you.

> Me: I know. Thanks though.

> Bryce: Anything for my girl.

I step out of the Uber. I could use my key to get up to Cooper's place, but this isn't the time for it, so I press the button on the buzzer.

"Who is it?" he answers.

"Let me up," I say, and the buzzer goes off for me to get past the gated door.

I don't have much time to prepare my words because, of course, Cooper being Cooper, he meets me outside his door, watching me climb the stairs. He's in jogger pants and nothing else as if maybe he was sleeping. Damn, why does he have to be such a temptation when I'm here to give him a piece of my mind?

CHAPTER 12
COOPER

For a second, I try to figure out how Ellery knows. She's got that pissed-off look that's usually associated with Dr. Murphy. But today it's aimed right at me.

"We need to talk." She walks right by me into my apartment. "And put a shirt on."

I grab a T-shirt from my bedroom drawer and throw it on, finding her pacing in front of my television. I pick up the remote and turn off the morning show I was watching.

"What's wrong?"

She stares at my hand, and I know for sure that she knows what happened last night. I haven't even looked on my phone yet to see if any videos have turned up.

Miles and Damon lectured me the entire ride back to the hotel. Thankfully, most people slept on the plane ride back this morning, so no one said anything, but I'd be naive to think there isn't footage out there somewhere showing me punching a teammate.

"Seriously? You're going to play stupid?" She stops pacing and crosses her arms. She's wearing yoga pants and a long-sleeve shirt with a puffy vest over it.

"I hit him." I spread my arms out as if I were asking if that's what she wanted to hear.

She balks, and her jaw hangs open as she stares at me. "Why would you do that?"

"Because he was all over another girl!" I'm not going to be made to feel stupid for what I did. I punched him for being a douchebag. For not knowing exactly what he has in his grip and for not cherishing her. "And he made a crude comment I didn't appreciate."

She squeezes the bridge of her nose and inhales deeply as if she needs to center herself. "Bradley and I aren't exclusive."

"So?"

"So you had no right to do what you did, and now there are videos out there. Everyone who knows us is going to assume it's over me. I can't go from always being videoed and photographed as your best friend, and then I start dating one of your teammates and suddenly you end up punching him. Do you know how humiliating this is for me?"

I head into my kitchen to make breakfast. "Did you think I'd just sit there and watch him be all over some girl when my entire team knows he's dating you?" I crack an egg and drop it in the bowl, throwing the shell away.

"It's none of your business," she says, coming to my side farther down the counter.

"And if roles were reversed?" I arch an eyebrow.

"You're missing the point. We weren't even boyfriend and girlfriend. I was just dating him. He was free to do what he wanted."

I'm baffled that we're even having this fight. She should be saying thank you, and that's the end of it. "It doesn't matter if he'd gone out with you once. The point is, as long as you are in his life, he shouldn't be fucking around with someone else. He should be head over heels for you."

Her fists tighten, and she strangles out a cry. "What aren't you understanding? I don't need you to be my bodyguard.

I'm not sure I can ever show my face again in front of your teammates."

"That's a tad dramatic," I say, continuing to crack eggs. "Let's just eat breakfast and forget the whole thing. I have more important problems coming my way from this fight. I might get suspended from games or benched. The coach hasn't called, but I'm waiting."

"More important?" she asks, cocking out her hip.

Oh fuck.

I sigh. "I'm gonna be honest, Elle, I don't understand why you're mad." I scramble the eggs, put some butter in a pan, and grab some veggies from the fridge.

"Because you're a man and you feel as if you handled it the right way? You gave him a black eye."

I stop what I'm doing and look at her. "How?"

"How what?" She paces again, her go-to when she wants to think clearly.

"How do you know he has a black eye? Is there a picture of it somewhere?"

She's quiet for a second.

My eyes narrow on her. "You saw him before coming here?" I dump the eggs in the pan and drop the bowl into the sink. It breaks into pieces from the force.

"Because *he* sent me a text this morning."

"To plead his case, Elle!"

"Yes, and he told me his side of the story at breakfast."

I stare at her in disbelief. This is how far apart we've gotten. "I can't believe you didn't come to me. You would've come to me before." I point at myself, my voice rising.

"And you wouldn't have hit him before! You would have been the one to tell me before!"

"Because you wouldn't have been dating him!"

"It's none of your business!" she shouts.

I close my eyes, my jaw tight. "Stop saying that."

"I've always respected the girls you hang out with," she says.

I give her my fakest laugh ever. "I never bring them around, plus I hardly date."

"Maybe you should. Maybe this whole best friend thing isn't working out anymore." She crosses her arms.

"You're not serious." There's no way she is.

Her hands fly up at her sides. "You clearly can't see how you crossed the line."

"And you clearly can't see why I would."

Both of our phones ding at the same time, and we each grab them.

> Bryce: Here you go. This is already live, nothing I could do.

Sure enough, it's a clip of the fight, and Ellery's face is at the top of the screen. The captions say she's responsible for our fight.

"Great. Just fucking great. Damn you, Cooper!"

She walks out of my door and slams it before I can stop her.

I decide not to chase after her because she needs to calm down. I unlock my screen to see a picture of Bradley with a black eye that someone must've taken this morning. My head rocks back. What the hell was I thinking? I've always been able to deal with my emotions like an adult.

That afternoon, I go to the office for the Chicago Grizzlies because Coach Stone has called me in. I'm not surprised when I walk into the waiting area and find Bradley sitting in a chair. His black eye isn't going to score me points with the coach.

I nod at Bradley. He's an idiot if he thinks I'm going to apologize.

"Happy you get her all to yourself now?" Bradley snipes.

I sit as far away from him as possible. "Why did you want to date her if you wanted to fuck around on her?"

"I wasn't fucking around on her, we weren't a committed couple. I'm not sure what you don't understand about that. She said she understood right before she dumped me at breakfast this morning."

I inwardly clap for Elle. "That's not the point. She's my best friend."

He scoffs.

"She is. We made a decision to just be friends a long time ago. But she's too good for someone who can't commit until you're having sex with her. That's the reason you were with that girl, right?"

His cheeks redden.

I figure I don't need to ask any more questions, I just need to tell him where it's at. "Ellery is the girl you cherish as soon as she says yes to dating you. The one you court, who gets all your attention, all your effort. The one who makes you feel blessed that she wants you. The one you'll wait forever for until she's ready. She's not the one you date at the same time as five other girls."

"It was a hookup. Jesus, Cooper." He rolls his eyes.

"Exactly! You shouldn't want to fuck up things with Elle."

He laughs and shakes his head. "Go see a therapist and figure out why you can't tell her how you feel. Why you're so scared of starting a relationship with her because you love her more than any friend."

Coach's door opens before I can respond. "Get in here, you two idiots."

We look at one another. I threw the first punch, so it'll all be on me. I wait for him to walk in first, then I follow, shutting the door.

"Nice shiner," Coach says, staring at me.

I bite the inside of my cheek. "I'm not apologizing."

"Sit down."

We both sit in the chairs across from him.

He runs his hand down his face. "This is ridiculous, you both know that, right? We're in what could be our third season going to the championship and you jackasses pull this stunt. Do I have to remind you who we play next week?"

"No, sir," we say in unison.

"The second-ranked team in the conference. And I wish it was up to me what happens with you two, but of course, the commissioner called me this morning."

I didn't think about all this before I went after Bradley.

"You're both suspended for one game," he says.

"I didn't even throw a punch," Bradley says, leaning forward.

"You know you're part of this, and you each have ten grand in fines." Coach Stone massages his temples. "I need to retire." He sighs. "From now on, please tell Ellery I am forbidding her to date anyone on the Grizzlies."

Bradley laughs. "You mean except for Cooper, right?"

"Yes, that was implied."

I shake my head. "Are we free to go now?"

"Bradley is, but you're staying." He turns to Bradley. "I'll be in touch if I hear anything more. Put some makeup on that thing or something."

"Okay, Coach." He rolls his eyes and leaves the room.

It's dead silent while I wait for Coach to start in on me.

He takes his time before he speaks. "I'm no psychologist, but you can't go apeshit every time someone hurts Ellery."

"I would've done it for Bryce, but now she's got Miles." I don't uncross my arms.

"With all of your ego and testosterone, I'm surprised you've made it this far. Just keep this shit out of the locker room. This is what I meant at the start of the season. Distractions aren't going to get you where you want to be at the end of the season. Do you want that third ring in consecutive years?"

"Hell yeah."

"Then stop this bullshit. If you want to date her, date her, but if not, then I'm sorry, but you don't get to be her bodyguard. She can handle herself."

I don't say anything because I don't agree.

"Whatever." He waves me off. "But you better use your free time to get Vetter up to speed for next week. We might not have you and Bradley, but we still need to win."

I nod. "I'll apologize to the team for putting them at a disadvantage this week, but not for the reason I did it."

He nods. "How's the hand? The knuckles." I hold up my hand, and he winces. "Damn, can you even throw?"

"It's just swollen. It'll go down."

He shakes his head. I hate that I've disappointed him. It feels like a physical weight on my shoulders.

"Make sure you see medical and see what they can do to speed up that recovery." He points at the door. "Now get out of my sight. I have to go buy my wife flowers and hope she forgives me for running out on her brunch this morning."

"Sorry," I say, cringing.

"Yeah, you fucked with my life, you should be." The tip-up of his lips says he forgives me though.

I walk out of the Grizzlies head office and get into my Land Rover. My thumb goes to call Ellery, but I change screens before pressing the button on my satellite radio.

Isn't this the exact type of thing we were trying to stay away from? Never in all these years have we fought like we did this morning. I saw it in her eyes—it's going to be a long time before she forgives me.

CHAPTER 13

ELLERY

AFTER COLLEGE GRADUATION

I was unpacking a box in Cooper's new apartment our senior year. He had decided to rent a place by Bryce and me. We'd had no romantic relationship because we were both so focused on our goals, and after his dad's speech at dinner that night, it'd been clear to me that romance wasn't in the cards for us. But we'd become the closest of friends.

His phone rang, and he answered, putting it on speaker as he took piles of clothes out of the boxes to put in his dressers. "Hey, Mom, before you ask, we got here ourselves. Ellery drove the truck."

"I did not," I said loudly enough for her to hear.

"Oh, Coop," she said, a sob racking through her. "I have something to tell you."

Cooper grabbed the phone and sat on the edge of the bed. "Mom?"

I sat next to him, my stomach pitching from the pain in his mom's voice.

"Hey, Coop, it's Uncle Henry. Your mom needs a moment."

"Why? What's going on? Where's Dad?" He looked at me in a panic, and I felt it in my gut. This was going to be one of those moments we would always remember.

"I'm sorry, kid, he had a heart attack this morning."

Cooper's eyes flared open then squeezed shut. "Is he okay? At the hospital?"

I'd heard it in his uncle's voice, but Cooper was probably in denial.

"No, he passed away. I'm sorry."

Cooper stared at the floor while tears streamed down my face. I couldn't wipe them away fast enough.

His uncle cleared his throat. "I'm going to call the airlines and get you a ticket home."

"Two tickets," Cooper said and looked at me.

God, it was the start of our senior year, and I was going to miss my first classes of the semester if I went with him. He had the excuse, it was his father, but who was I except for emotional support? Regardless, I had to be with him, so I nodded.

"For Ellery?" his uncle asked, having met me when he came up last year to visit.

"Yes," Cooper said.

"Okay, I'll let you know the arrangements as soon as I have them." He paused for a while, and we heard a door shut. "Listen, kid, your mom… she's a mess. She wanted to tell you herself, but she's still absorbing it all. I'm sure once she sees you, the two of you can grieve, but if you need anything, call me."

"Thanks, Uncle Henry," Cooper said, but I'm not sure if he even heard his uncle. He seemed to be somewhere else in his head.

"I'll be in touch."

They hung up, and I slid closer to Cooper, taking his hand and squeezing to let him know I was there.

He had no tears in his eyes as he stared at me for a long moment. "He'll never see me get drafted. Never see me make the pros."

I squeezed his hand. "He will. He just won't be sitting next to you."

"Let's get packed. I have to call Coach."

For the rest of the day, he unpacked his apartment and packed his suitcase. We returned the rental truck, and he called his coach. Uncle Henry called two hours later with our flight arrangements. We had to be in Missouri in two days for his father's funeral.

Two days later, the plane landed at the Missouri airport. Cooper was more of a zombie than anything, and I didn't have the right words to say. What kind of doctor was I going to be if I had no bedside manner?

We got our luggage, Uncle Henry picked us up in his truck, and we headed to Cooper's childhood home.

Once we were at the front door, his uncle turned to us. "We set up the two bedrooms. Your mother should be back soon. She's with Aunt Helen, getting her hair done."

Cooper laughed, but his uncle gave him a look that made him stop.

"Ellery, you can sleep in the guest room." Henry took my bag up the stairs to the room next to Cooper's childhood room.

"No, she's staying with me." Cooper grabbed my suitcase and put it in his room.

"Coop…" I said. Sure, we'd slept in the same bed before, but usually because there was no other option.

"I need you with me."

The pain in his voice got to me, and I gave his uncle a wan

smile, unsure what to do. I'd been with Cooper for the past two nights at school, but once he fell asleep, I'd slipped out and gone back to my apartment.

"Your mom probably won't even notice, plus you're adults." He went downstairs.

I went into Cooper's room. "Are you crazy? We don't want to upset anyone."

"I don't give a shit. I don't want to be alone." His tone was final, and I wasn't going to upset him even more than he already was.

I sat on his burgundy comforter and examined his room. There were trophies everywhere. Talk about a high school jock's room. Posters of cars—Corvettes mostly—and famous quarterbacks. He shut the door to his bedroom, and on the wall behind the door was a collage of pictures, mostly of his dad when he played professional football.

Cooper flopped down on the bed. "I'm tired. Join me for a nap?"

Things had shifted since the news of his father's death. Cooper was much more touchy-feely than before. I crawled up to his headboard and rested my back against it. He rested his head in my lap and wrapped his arm around my waist. My hand strayed to his hair, my fingers combing through it. I had no idea what to do or how to make this better for him, so I let him lead and I followed, hoping we weren't going to end up somewhere we shouldn't.

———

I'd admit, I'd been to very few funerals before Cooper's dad, but it was the saddest event I'd ever experienced.

His mom couldn't stop crying, and his aunt Helen tried to console her to no avail.

Cooper never let my hand go, even when someone

hugged him and gave him their condolences, which made it even more awkward. I got a lot of looks from people wondering who I was until Cooper introduced me as his best friend.

His dad's closest friends, who happened to be from the teams he'd played for, all flew in and told stories of their times on the road. The preacher said some thoughtful things, and when it was Cooper's turn, I thought I'd be going up there with him, but he squeezed my hand and walked to the podium by himself.

The room appeared to become even more somber as Cooper cleared his throat. He stood in front of the big picture of his dad when he was probably about Cooper's age, playing in the league. It was like looking at a real-life replica—except for those dark eyes that held so much grief. I wondered how long it took a person to pull out of the sadness of losing a loved one. Did they ever?

"My dad and I didn't always see eye to eye." Cooper locked eyes with me and held my gaze for a second. "He always pushed me to be better. There was no going to eat after a game, only practicing to improve what I did wrong. I spent more time in the gym than any other teammate, and sometimes I had to do it again with my dad when I got home. People probably thought he was living vicariously through me, but he wanted me to have what he did. His time in the league were the best years of his life. He told me that constantly." Cooper's gaze found his mom at that moment, and she stopped crying.

I suddenly wasn't so sure this was a normal eulogy.

"He loved us, we know he did, but the game of football... well, he fell in love with that first. He trained me because he loves the game. That's all it comes down to. I'm not sure he ever fully retired, but I have him to thank for the player I am today. He saw me win Player of the Year last year, and as my best friend Ellery told me, he'll see me be drafted this year, just from a different view. I love my dad for everything he was and everything he wasn't to me. He just couldn't turn off the switch, and I think there were times he felt guilty for that. But it's okay, Dad, we forgive you. Half of what we loved about you was your love for the sport. Rest in peace. You taught me well, and I can take over on our dream now."

He walked down the stairs of the church, and his mom stood and wrapped her arms around her son. It was the first hug I'd seen them exchange since we'd arrived. But it was Cooper's back shaking as he cried in his mom's arms that spurred my own tears. Having a complicated relationship with my own father, I understood how you could love them so much, faults and all.

After the funeral, when everyone went back to their house, Cooper pulled me away to a garage out back. He pressed a button, and the garage door opened. Inside were four cars, but he didn't focus on the other three. He went right over to a cherry-red Corvette.

His hand ran along the hood. "My dad and I restored this one together."

"It's really nice." I found a chair and sat down. Between all the emotions and feeling weird sleeping in the same bed as Cooper, I was exhausted.

"My mom told me to take it back with me, but I think I'll wait until I get drafted. I don't want anything to happen to it."

"That's nice of her."

He huffed. "She doesn't want anything. She just wants him, and it's the one thing she can't have."

"I can imagine."

I watched as he opened the passenger door and signaled for me to get in. I climbed in, and he shut the door before going to the other side. Once he slid in next to me, he turned on the car and rolled down the windows. The music was low, and I waited for him to put it in drive, but his hand never went to the shifter.

"My mom used to show up at his hotels when the team traveled. She went to every home game and stayed after, leaving me with a babysitter. When he was too far away and she couldn't go, she'd call him constantly."

I didn't know if he wanted me to say something, so I kept quiet, and he continued.

"He was her entire life. More important than even me."

"Oh, Cooper," I said, not agreeing.

"No, he was, and I made peace with that a long time ago. It was good because I would've cracked if they both were looking at me under a microscope. She was so paranoid that he was cheating on her." He looked at me. "I think it's why I don't want to be one of those players who sleeps with a bunch of people."

"You think your dad…"

He nodded. "I do. He cheated on his first wife with my mom—that's why my mom was so paranoid. But I'll never know. His friends would never tell me, and I don't blame them. My dad was the good-time guy, you know? Life of the party."

I squeezed his hand.

"I never want my wife to feel that way, but I've seen the worst in the league. I've seen what being married to a player can strip from someone. It stripped my mother of being who she was meant to be, and I never want that to happen to…"

He didn't finish, and I was desperate to know if he wanted to end that sentence with the word *you*. Because I wanted to rebut. I wanted to tell him that I would have my career, and I trusted him. But it all came back to our hang-ups that kept us from crossing over that friendship line.

Cooper put his hand on the shifter as the song "Wind of Change" by the Scorpions came on. He drove the car out of the garage through his parents' rural neighborhood, and we didn't speak a word. We just listened to music and drove with the wind running through our hair. It was the most freeing moment of my life because I stopped thinking about everything. Nothing mattered more than that exact moment in time.

CHAPTER 14

COOPER

"Why are we doing this again?" I ask Damon, who hijacked me after practice.

"Because it's fun," Miles says from the other side of me.

The three of us are in the back of the smallest Uber in the world since the driver said he didn't want anyone sitting in the front with him. We sit shoulder to shoulder with no need for seat belts because there's no way any of us will shift around if we get in an accident.

"Next time get an Uber XL, man," I say to Damon.

"I forgot, okay? It's not that long of a ride." Damon types away on his phone.

"How did I get stuck in the middle?" I grumble.

"Jesus, stop complaining already. You owe us. Your temper got you suspended, which means we might lose on Sunday, so you just need to sit there and look pretty." Damon taps my knee.

"I'm assuming Elle will be there?" We had all talked about trying curling before, so if they think they're surprising me with her being there and keeping me locked in the middle seat, they worried for nothing.

"Of course, those are the couples," Damon says, not looking away from his phone.

"I'm not part of a couple." I shift in my seat, what little I can.

"You never minded before," Miles says. "In fact, you were more of a couple with Ellery than any of us at one point."

"That's changed." I'm purposely being an asshole because she's still mad at me. Granted, I haven't reached out to her. But I don't think I have to. I did nothing wrong.

"Don't we all know it. It's like we're the kids caught in the middle of Mommy and Daddy's divorce." Damon shakes his head at me, finally looking up from his phone.

We pull up to the big building, and I'm thankful to be here. The sooner we get inside, the sooner I can get this over with.

Heading into the building, I'll admit I'm a little excited to try something I've only ever seen on television during the Olympics. Damon takes charge, heading over to the desk to get us registered. The women come out from the bar. Elle sips her drink, giving me a fake smile around her straw, while Bryce and Adeline both greet me with a hug.

Damon comes back over and joins the group. "Okay, so it's groups of four, so we're paired up with another couple. They said we could go down to the curling lane. They're already there."

"Great." I fake excitement.

Miles puts his hand on my neck and squeezes, detouring us away from the others toward the curling lanes. "Get a grip, Cooper. We're here for fun, and if you sour this for all of us, *I'm* going to punch *you* in the face."

"And get suspended? That would be irresponsible."

He rolls his eyes before he walks over to Bryce, smacking her on the ass. She squeals, and he wraps her arms around him.

I sit on the bench as Damon introduces us to the cute

couple waiting there, Kit and Kevin. Apparently, they're newly married. They both have blond hair and blue eyes and look oddly alike.

"We have to split up, and we cannot give that happy couple Elle and Coop," Bryce says, looking at me and Ellery, who is on the opposite side of the bench and sucking the last drop of her drink through her straw.

"Not on call tonight?" I ask.

"Nope." She goes back to sucking.

"You're going to blow a blood vessel, get another drink."

She scowls at me. "I will when I'm ready." She picks up the straw and moves it around the ice.

"Seriously, want me to buy one for you?"

"Maybe I don't want another one?"

"Whatever," I mumble. All of our friends are staring at us when I look up. "What?"

They shake their heads.

"We'll couple up with Kit and Kevin," Damon says.

"Hell no, we're flipping for it," Bryce says.

"I don't think they're flipping, hoping they get us," I say to Ellery, who shrugs.

"I wouldn't want to be on your team anyway," she says to me.

What the hell? That hurts more than it probably should.

They flip a coin, and Miles and Bryce end up on Kit and Kevin's team.

"We're trading if they don't snap out of it," Damon says to Miles.

"Are you guys..." Kevin gets his broom. "Football players?"

I sigh.

The woman points at me. "You're Cooper Rice, right?"

A sound comes from Ellery, and I turn to her. "What?"

"Just not surprising that she knows you, Mister Endorsement."

I arch an eyebrow at her. "Meaning?"

"Ever heard of the word no? You wonder why you're everywhere? You put yourself there."

"Fucking hell," Damon grumbles and looks at Kit and Kevin. "Excuse the bickering duo over there."

"Is it because of the video?" Kit asks in an unsure voice.

I strip my gaze off Ellery to look at Kit.

Ellery laughs. "Why, yes, it is." Ellery smiles and gets up, going over to talk to Adeline about what roles each of us should have on the team.

"I'm just gonna assign ours," Damon says. "Adeline and Ellery, you two sweep, I guide the rock, and Cooper is the captain telling us what to do."

Both of the girls put their hands on their hips and stare him down.

"Um… no," Adeline says.

"Why would Cooper be the captain?" Ellery asks.

Damon looks at me with an expression that says he thinks coming here was a big mistake. "He's the captain of the team. He's used to being a leader."

"I work in the chaos of the ER," Ellery says.

"I run a classroom of middle schoolers," Adeline says.

"Fine." Damon holds up his hands in obvious defeat.

"We'll draw for the positions." Adeline grabs a piece of paper and a pen from her purse.

We pull the spots and lucky us, Ellery and I are the sweepers, Adeline will be captain, and Damon gets to guide the rock.

This should be fun.

We manage to finish curling without fighting anymore. Occasionally, Ellery wanted her broom first and started overpowering me, but I didn't fight her too much.

We say goodbye to Kit and Kevin, exchanging numbers so we can get them tickets to a home game, and head to the restaurant at the curling place. It isn't fancy, but it's quiet because there's hardly anyone here, and they only play curling on the television, not sports or entertainment news.

Ellery and I sit across from one another, with each couple on our sides. I feel like the damn mom and dad of the crew. We order our meals, and the table is unusually quiet. I hate the fact I'm not talking with Elle unless we're arguing.

"So, Adeline and I have an announcement!" Damon interrupts the awkward silence and stands.

I can only imagine what he has to say. Another baby, maybe? Which would mean he's got two and I've got none. Not even a wife.

I used to think I didn't want a relationship while I was in the league. The hell it put my mother through, I never wanted that for anyone. But as I grew up and saw what being in the league was like, I figured out quickly that I'm not my dad. And a lot of the guys aren't like my dad's old school buddies.

The problem is there's only one person I want a life with if I'm honest with myself, and that woman currently doesn't want anything to do with me.

"Our bye week is coming, and originally, I wanted to take my girl away, but we've decided we want all of us to go up to a cabin. We're going to leave Clover with her grandparents. I found the perfect cabin where we can ski, downhill or cross country, or we can ice skate and do all kinds of outdoor activities."

"First of all, we can't ski during football season," I say. The fact we played curling might not be great, but it's not high-risk like skiing.

"Okay, buzzkill, well, there's a lot we can do up there in Wisconsin, and it'll be so much fun. A getaway I think we all need."

"I love the thought, but I'm out," Ellery says.

Damon looks at Adeline as if she needs to do something. Adeline stares back at him as though he's suggesting she kidnap Ellery.

"Okay, I'm gonna be honest," Damon says. "This whole situation between you two blows. You're sucking the fun out of everything for all of us. Grow up, talk about the problem." He sits down and crosses his arms.

"Grow up? I'm being a grown-up. I'm here, aren't I?" Ellery says. "I could have canceled on all of this, but you're asking me to go away with him when he's not even apologetic for what he did."

"Why should I be? I did it for your honor."

"Oh please, my honor." She shakes her head.

"Forget this shit." I stand.

Miles quickly rises to his feet and presses me back down with his hand on my shoulder. "Listen. We didn't want to tell anyone this, but this trip needs to be now, even if you guys aren't getting along."

"Miles?" Bryce shakes her head.

"We have to," he says, turning to all of us. "Bryce and I want to have a baby, and this is a great opportunity for her to have some fun before we really start trying."

Ellery's head whips in her friend's direction. "Seriously?" There's a look on her face that resembles yearning, as if she wants a family too.

Bryce nods. "I'm asking for one last trip before, you know."

Ellery looks across the table at me, and our gazes hold. We can't be the two holdouts because of our bickering.

Bryce's head volleys between Ellery and me. "Please, you two. Can you put these differences aside this one time?"

"The four of you can go. We won't be much fun anyway," I answer. "We'll ruin it."

Bryce shakes her head. "It's not the same. You guys have

been with me since college, and I want you both there." She gives Ellery her pouty look that works every time.

"I'll go," Ellery says.

"Figures." I sigh.

"And now you? Please, Cooper?"

I think about it for a moment. "How many bedrooms are there?"

"Four beds, four baths so it's perfect." Damon smiles and looks at Miles as though they did good.

"Fine, but we're all driving up together?"

"Yeah, for sure," Miles says.

"Yay! Let's have a shot to celebrate." Bryce goes over to the bar and talks to the bartender.

Glad at least one of us is happy.

CHAPTER 15

COOPER

Two weeks later, I'm standing on the curb outside The Den with Ellery and our rental van, but the other four are missing in action.

"That's it, I'm sending a text." I push my hand into the pocket of my coat and pull out my phone.

> Me: Where are you all? ETA?

Bryce: I got held up getting a snowsuit at the mall. They're trying to find the one I ordered to be delivered. Miles is with me. We'll be there soon.

Damon: We'll have to meet you guys there. Clover isn't having it, and Adeline is having the whole 'my baby wants me' moment. We'll get there tonight, but by the time we get back from the burbs, it's gonna be pretty late.

Adeline: I'm going to ignore you saying that so that we can have a nice weekend.

> Damon: I feel the same. I don't like to see her cry either. It breaks me.

> Miles: Bryce is delusional. We aren't getting out of here for another half hour and then the traffic into the city. We can detour around the city and probably beat you there. You two go on your own, and we'll see you there.

"What the hell!" I shout. "Tell me why I rented a damn minivan then?"

"Let's just go. I don't want to be driving in the dark. I've heard too many deer stories." Ellery climbs into the passenger seat.

"So, I'm the driver?" I point at myself.

"As if the captain would have it any other way." She slams the door.

I grunt and talk to myself the whole way around the van. "What happened to 'I'm the captain of the ER department'?"

I start the van, then put on my seat belt and ease into the traffic. It's going to be hell to get up to Wisconsin now that we've waited so long to leave. When we're stopped in traffic two minutes into our journey, I sigh, and Ellery looks over at me.

"Can we just not?" She puts in her earbuds and turns her head away from me to look out the window.

What the hell has happened to us?

I use the opportunity to listen to my music, following the directions on the GPS. I forgot how much fun it was to sing along to music while cruising around. It's been a while since I've done it. I can't roll down the windows because it's grown colder now, but it's still relaxing.

"I have to pee," she says, taking out her earbuds.

We pull off at the next exit and stop at a gas station. Each of us grabs some snacks, and when we get back in the van, I'm reminded of the trips we used to take. One of us always got licorice, and the other got chips. Somehow without us talking about it, it always happened.

She climbs in the car, and she's got licorice and chips. So much for us sharing, I guess. I look at my licorice in the center console, and she must be thinking the same thing as me. "You can have some of my chips if you'd like."

"No, I'm fine." I start the van and continue on our way.

She puts in her earbuds, and again, I'm left alone with my music.

Her perfume fills the car, and I don't even mind. She's usually not one to wear it, at least when it comes to work. Maybe she wears it all the time now. How the hell would I know?

These past three weeks have been complete torture. I've picked up the phone more than once to call her but never followed through.

I glance at her as I exit the freeway. We have another twenty-minute drive off the highway to get to the cabin.

How can she be that mad at me for punching Bradley? I must be missing something. I've done other stupid things throughout our friendship, and she never stopped talking to me for this long. Then again, I was quick to apologize for those. In this instance, I honestly don't think I did anything wrong.

A text comes through, and Ellery pulls it up on her phone. "Miles says they hit traffic, and Damon sent the code for us to get in the cabin. Said there should be essentials for eating."

"Great."

Ten minutes later, we pull up in front of a cabin. It's nicely tucked away in the woods. I can see the neighbor, but they aren't super close. I park the van in the driveway and turn off the ignition. I examine the house for a minute and wonder where the hell four bedrooms and four baths could possibly be because it doesn't look that big.

Ellery exits the van and shuts the door before opening up the back and taking out her luggage. She wheels it up to the door and uses the code to get in. It's decorated much like I'd expect from a Wisconsin cabin. A big deer head on the wall, a stone fireplace, and wood floors. Other than that, it's like a log cabin.

"Are we sure this is it? I don't see how there could be four bedrooms," she says.

I follow her into the kitchen and find a note on the counter. She picks it up and opens it while I look in the fridge to see that it's stocked and even has a bottle of champagne.

"I think this was for someone else." I show her the bottle of champagne, and she frowns and glances back down at the note.

"'Ellery and Cooper,'" she says with a pissed-off expression. The fact that the letter is just to us cements my assumption that this is a one-bedroom cabin with probably one bed. "'We love you both and apologize for tricking you, but to be blunt, you two need to get your shit together. As your oldest friend, I'm telling you, the two of you mean a helluva lot more to each other than just a best friend. I get that you're scared. I was scared. Miles was scared. Both Damon and Adeline were scared. Everyone who risks their heart is scared. And I get it, I understand that you guys don't want to risk your friendship. But where is your friendship now? You guys are lying to yourselves and it's hurting you. Don't even get me started on this ridiculous fight you guys are in. So, you have all weekend to figure it out. I know what I'm hoping for, but I'll take you two making up at the very least…'"

We hear the sound of a car engine, and I look out the window to see the minivan pulling away.

Ellery groans but keeps reading. "'You're by yourselves with two nights to find your way back to one another. Use the time wisely. And please be honest with yourselves. We love you. Bryce and the gang.'" She drops the letter on the counter. "Isn't this great?" She picks up her phone and presumably dials Bryce. "Her voicemail."

She hangs up and sits down in the chair.

I peruse the rest of the cabin, and sure enough, there's one bed, one bath.

"Well, I'm going to make dinner," I say.

"I'm not hungry."

I slam the fridge. "Since when are you not hungry?"

She shrugs. "Since now."

I stomp over to her, annoyed and pissed off. "We're gonna talk."

"I don't have anything to say."

"What are you, five, and having a temper tantrum? Get over here. We're finishing this now."

"Five? *You* acted like you were five. Someone else was playing with your toy so you punched him in the face." Her voice escalates.

Though I hate how mad she is, I'm just happy to get a reaction out of her.

"Toy? That's what you think you are to me?"

"That's how I felt when I found out about the fight. You're not a normal guy, Cooper. You're Cooper Rice, quarterback for the Chicago Grizzlies. It's embarrassing and makes me think people assume I'm playing two guys. I can't wait until the slut comments start hitting social media." She runs her hand down her face. "You went after him with the excuse that it was for me, but in reality, it was for you because of your red rage."

I open my mouth, but she continues. "I get it, okay? I hear people all the time talk shit about your performance, and as soon as I tell them you're my friend, they shut up, but instead of attacking them, I tell them about the kind-hearted person you are. I stick up for you. But what you did at that bar…" She shakes her head as though she's disappointed in me.

"You're right." I go to start the pilot light on the gas fireplace, feeling way too vulnerable to let her see inside me right now. "I saw red. I wanted to beat the shit out of him. I'm happy Damon and Miles got me off of him when they did."

She sits quietly on the plaid couch, bringing her legs under her. "Do you see how weak it made me feel? I had two adult men fighting, and not over me. I've caught hell at work, but it's died down."

I light the gas for the fireplace and sit back to make sure it's good before heading over to the couch with her since the chair looks too small to be comfortable for me. I'm starting to think this cabin is designed for people who need to make up after a fight. "I'm sorry."

"Would you have done that if it was Bryce or Adeline?"

"You can't even compare, and you know it."

She picks at the blanket, her gaze seeming unwilling to meet mine. "Why? Why am I different?"

I lean forward and rest my forearms on my thighs. My head hangs, and I stare at the hardwood floor. "You don't want me to tell you."

My chest constricts because if I do this, if I say the words out loud, there's no going back. I could be taking our friendship and sending it careening off a cliff.

"Tell me."

My chest squeezes even more, and there's this painful ache where my heart is. I glance at her from the corner of my eye. "You have to be sure."

"I think Bradley stirred some things up between us. Things maybe we've both been feeling but haven't been saying."

"Elle." I sigh. "We promised one another." My voice is a pained whisper.

She nods. "I know we did, but words and promises don't change what our hearts feel."

"It will change everything between us." I shake my head.

"We're at a crossroads here, Coop. We can't keep pretending we're those naive college kids anymore." She pulls the blanket tighter around her.

I toe out of my shoes and turn on the couch to face her. My outstretched arm almost reaches her. I want it to. I want to touch her and kiss her and love her until she won't let me anymore. God, just talking to her again feels so good already.

"I was pissed at Bradley because he had you. He had you, and he disrespected you by dancing with that woman. And he was going to sleep with her, mark my words."

She nods. "Probably. But it wasn't your job to put him in line. I'm afraid you see me as a stand-in for your mom."

My eyes cut to her. What is she talking about? "My mom?"

"That's why you went after him. It reminded you of your mom and dad. How your mom was so afraid of your dad cheating on her that she'd show up at road games and surprise him. There you were on the road and saw the guy I'm dating dancing with another woman."

"Fuck." I run my hand through my hair. I never even thought of it that way before. Never put those things together.

"I'm not your mom," she whispers.

"I know that."

"Do you?" Wetness fills her eyes.

I pause before I respond. "I had my suspicions about how the league worked from stories my dad told me. The women everywhere throwing themselves at you. I never wanted someone I cared about to have to deal with that or feel insecure about it." I stop, the realization gutting me. "I think I tried to be content with us staying in the best friend zone to prevent you from ever feeling that pain I saw my mom live through all those years, but…"

"Someone else did it anyway. You tried to save me from it, but someone else did it. Or so you thought."

"Shit, Elle." I scoot closer to her. "You're right. That's why I'm so mad about it. All this time, I've kept my feelings hidden to keep you safe."

"You were forgetting one thing, Cooper."

"What?"

She places her hand on my stubbled cheek. "I'd only ever hurt like that if you did it to me. I never cared about Bradley, not in that way. And even if I had, it would never measure up to how much I care about you."

"Are you saying what I think you are?"

She gives me a coy smile. "That depends. Do you have something to tell me?"

I freeze, stuck in my fear again. I've already pretty much told her without saying the words, but as soon as the words come out of my mouth, they're there, lying between us, never to be taken back.

Can I break the promise I made to her eight years ago? I'm not sure.

CHAPTER 16

ELLERY

SENIOR YEAR OF COLLEGE

Bryce and I were meeting Cooper at a party. Unfortunately, he hadn't won the Player of the Year award that year, even though he'd won it the previous year, but he wasn't upset. His eyes were on the future, with the draft only months away. With the help of the coaches and his dad's friends, he found an agent he really connected with.

Things were going well. Although sometimes I saw the grief of missing his dad seep in, most of the time, he was the same old Cooper.

"Do I look okay?" Bryce asked while we walked down the sidewalk toward the party.

It wasn't hard to find the house with the noise flowing down to the street. She was wearing a short skirt and a tight T-shirt that showed off her body. She'd recently broken up with Ian and was searching for a rebound.

"You look great."

She hooked her arm in mine as we walked. "You know, Cooper seems different lately."

"How so?"

"I think he might be ready to be more than friends. Now that some time has passed since his dad died."

Some people filed down onto the sidewalk with drunken swaggers as we grew closer to the house.

"I'm not sure about that."

There had been more than one time when I'd thought that maybe we'd both had enough of just friendship. Late nights of studying where we woke up cuddled on the couch. Or watching movies with our legs or arms touching, causing electricity to shoot up my arm. Sometimes I felt like I was the only one who felt that way. But last week, he cornered me in the galley kitchen and tickled me until I screamed mercy. It ended with me bending back on the counter and him right above me, chest to chest. Our eyes locked, and in that instant, I knew that I wasn't the only one thinking about what it would be like if we were more than friends.

"You know it scares him." I'd told her what had happened at his dad's funeral in the Corvette. He was scared to make someone he cared about crazy with paranoia that he was cheating on him.

"I'm not so sure. Would a friend wait on the porch?"

I followed her line of vision and found Cooper talking to someone on the porch. He was casually leaning against one of the pillars, smiling and laughing. The pit of my stomach said there was a reason our lives had intertwined all along.

"Jeez, look at you. I'm so jealous."

"We're friends," I said, approaching the walkway to the house.

Cooper said goodbye to whoever he was talking to and met us at the top of the stairs.

"Delusional friends. I gotta go find a man. Hey, Coop." Bryce hugged him and went into the house.

"What's with her?" he asked, glancing over his shoulder.

"Looking for a rebound to get her mind off Ian."

He opened his arms, and I stepped into them, allowing the warmth of his body to replace the chill in mine from walking down the block.

"Well, Ian is here, so this should be interesting." Cooper released me, but his hand slid into mine. "Let's get a drink."

We weaved through the crowd of people talking, dancing, and drinking until we reached the kitchen. We opted to get beers from the keg and found a spot in the living room to talk. Some of his teammates came by and said hello to us, but Cooper was quick to dismiss them, even though we usually socialized with everyone.

He sat on the ledge of the windowsill while I stood between his legs. It was more intimate than we usually were with each other, but it felt nice. As I sipped my beer, I almost choked it out when his hand landed on the back of my thigh, running up and down as if we were a couple already.

My stomach fluttered like hummingbird wings, and I turned to face him. "Whatcha doing?"

He set down his beer and stood to his full height, towering over me by six inches. Both of his hands fell to my hips. "Want to dance?"

"Since when do you dance?" I chuckled.

He leaned close, and my breath hitched when I thought he might kiss me. "Since right now."

After taking my beer from my hand, he placed it next to his. As if we were ever going back to get them. With his hand in mine again, he guided me to the middle of the dance floor, pulled me into his arms, and locked me against his chest. God, it felt good, there was no denying that.

The music was slow, easy to dance to, and our emotions rose to the surface.

"Elle," he whispered, moving my hair over my shoulder. "I've been thinking…"

Oh boy, this was it. He was going to make this a thing. Did I want it to be a thing? Did I want us to be involved romantically? Part of me said yes. Take him back to my apartment to feel those lips on mine and what those strong hands and fingers could do to my body. But I didn't want us waking up the next morning and looking at one another as though we'd made a mistake.

"Yes?" My mind was still whirling, but I needed to answer him.

"We're about to graduate. I don't know where I'm headed yet. There's a lot of talk about who wants me, but nothing's for sure. You're going to Chicago for medical school."

"It's a lot of change." I wasn't looking forward to the days when he would no longer be my neighbor.

His breath tickled the soft spot right under my earlobe. "Yeah, and this is probably our last opportunity to be with one another." He linked his hands behind my back, and my breasts crushed against his strong chest.

"But then we'll have to leave each other," I reminded him in case he'd forgotten that while we might have a couple of months now, what happened after graduation?

"What if we threw caution to the wind and just said fuck all the reasons we've kept our relationship to only being friends?" He drew back to see my expression.

I tried my hardest to fight the fear racing through me. I wanted to cross the line, but his dad had shut that down shortly after we met, and after he'd died, Cooper became distant and seemed to double down on that sentiment, so this Cooper? He was all new to me.

"I never want to lose you in my life," I said.

Which was the truth. Cooper meant so much more to me than sex and my attraction to him. He listened to me and knew me well enough that just from me saying hello, he'd know if it was a good day or bad. On the bad days, he always brought me his homemade chocolate chip cookies. We'd woven our friendship into the fabric of our lives, and I would have been devastated if we tried our luck at romance and it made us worse, not better.

He brushed back my hair, tucking it behind my ear. "You'll never lose me. Ever."

"You say that now, but we've all seen what happens when relationships go south. You forget all the things you used to like about each other." Maybe I was being selfish, but there was already so much change happening in the coming months. I wasn't sure I wanted this to change too. "It's already going to be so hard to say goodbye to one another when you get drafted to some team on the West Coast and I'm in Chicago."

He laughed, and his eyes met mine. For a second, he said nothing. "One thing I love about you is your ability to overthink something. These are our last few months before we have to go out into the real world and be adults. I want to do that with you as my girlfriend and not as my best friend. Think about it... lazy Sundays in bed after a night of fucking, I make you breakfast in bed. Walks through campus hand in hand, being able to kiss each other whenever we want. You coming with me to the draft, and we get a hotel room to celebrate after."

I couldn't deny that he was getting me closer and closer to agreeing to put everything we had in jeopardy. "Are you sure you shouldn't be rethinking a career in law?"

He chuckled. "What do you say?"

I smiled and bit my lip while fear pressed down on me from all sides. But I pushed it away and went with the thread of a feeling that was always there, whether I wanted it to be or not—the one that made me think that Cooper and I could be something really special.

So I nodded. "Okay, okay, yeah." I sucked in a cleansing breath. It was done. I'd made my decision. But now that I knew I was probably about to have sex with Cooper, I needed a minute to get myself together. Freshen up and make sure I was perfect. "But I have to go to the bathroom first. I'll be right back."

He grinned at me, and his dimples came out, making the space between my thighs tingle in anticipation. "I'll find Bryce and tell her we're leaving."

I nodded. "Okay."

His eyes fell down my body, and my libido ignited from his attention. Yeah, we were going to do this.

I headed to the bathroom, but the line downstairs was way too long, so I went upstairs. There were only two people in line when I got there. Perfect.

By the time it was my turn, I was barely paying attention, wondering what it would feel like to be with Cooper after all this time. Questions racked my brain—what kind of lover was he? Would he treat me with gentle hands or be rough? Maybe a mixture of both?

I walked into the bathroom and turned the lock. My mind was consumed with everything Cooper. A cheesy smile reflected at me in the mirror when I washed my hands.

Bryce was going to flip after she found out we'd crossed the line.

"Fire!" someone screamed from the hallway, banging on the door.

"What?" Panic constricted my chest.

Okay. Okay. Calm down.

I touched the doorknob like we'd been taught as kids, and it was hot, which meant the fire was nearby. Heading to the small window by the toilet, I stood on top of the lid and opened the window. Flames came out of the window to my right, the wind making the flames leap into the night like outstretched fingers.

Shit. How the hell was I going to get out of here?

My phone rang in my pocket, Cooper's name on the screen. "Hello?"

"Where are you? I went to the bathroom." It was clear

from his voice that he was panicked, and I heard chaos surrounding him.

"I'm upstairs. The line was too long on the main floor, but I think the fire is up here."

"I'll come up and get you."

"*No!*" I screeched. "I think the fire is in the room next door."

"I'm coming." He hung up.

I had to get out of there before he risked himself. I took a towel and used it to cover the doorknob, tugging on the door until it inched back. Flames blazed over the doorways of the bedrooms, smoke billowing everywhere. A group of four were rushing to the stairs, and one girl grabbed my arm and pulled me in behind her.

Surely I'd see Cooper coming up, and he'd follow me downstairs, where we'd be safe.

The farther down the hallway I got, the smokier it became. I heard people screaming and crying. I touched the wall, almost tripping on a stair, and when I reached the landing at the bottom, all the people in front of me were gone.

"COOPER!" I yelled.

"ELLE!" he yelled back, but I couldn't figure out where his voice was coming from.

"I'm almost out. Meet me outside!" I screamed over all the confusion.

"GO! GO!" he yelled.

The firefighters arrived as I got outside, and one of them escorted me to the neighbor's yard.

"Elle!" Bryce rushed over. "Are you okay?"

"She needs to get checked out as soon as another ambulance gets here," the firefighter said to Bryce.

"Cooper," I said, and the firefighter looked down at me. "Our friend Cooper is in there. He was looking for me."

"Cooper Rice?" he asked.

Of course he knew Cooper. "Yes!"

"Shit." He walked away and talked into his radio, and I watched as two more firefighters entered the burning house.

Bryce sat next to me. Our hands tightened around each other's as we watched them bring out student after student, but none of them were Cooper.

"B, what if—"

"No. Don't let your mind go there. Don't. He's the fittest of anyone in there. He's going to make it out."

My stomach bottomed out, and my entire body went numb when a firefighter came out carrying Cooper and running toward an ambulance.

An hour later, I'd been checked out to make sure I hadn't taken in too much smoke, and Bryce and I were at the hospital in one of the ER rooms, waiting for Cooper to get back from a CT scan.

"I saw you two on the dance floor," Bryce says to me.

"That doesn't matter now." I started pacing again. I hadn't been able to stop it since we got here.

Bryce went to the vending machines, and a few minutes later, Cooper was wheeled in. He looked pretty good except for the soot covering him.

"Let him rest," the nurse said to me after getting him comfortable.

When she left the room, I grabbed his hand, tears running down my cheeks. "I was so scared."

"Me too," he said and squeezed my hand. "But we're good."

I shook my head, unable to even imagine how I would have dealt with it if the worst had happened. Who would know exactly what I needed on a bad day, and who would I celebrate with on the great days? "Promise me something?"

He stared into my eyes, that cocky smirk in place, both his dimples showing. "Promise what?"

"That you'll always be in my life. You'll never leave me."

"Come here," he said, and I crawled into the bed with him. "I'm fine. Look at me."

I did.

"I'm one hundred percent fine. It was just a scare."

"Just promise," I said, laying my head on his chest, desperate to hear him say the words.

"Okay, I promise." He wrapped his arm around me.

"Then it's settled." I sat up. "We're friends. Best friends until the end and nothing more. I can't risk losing you."

His eyebrows furrowed, and he studied me for a long while. Still not looking completely convinced, he nodded. "I promise."

"Thank you." I squeezed his body to mine. "Thank you."

CHAPTER 17

ELLERY

"That depends. Do you have something to tell me?" I ask Cooper.

My heart beats harder as I wait for him to answer. We've denied this for so long. I'm the one who made him promise we'd only ever be friends because I was so scared. The feeling of losing him was too great to bear, but after Bradley put a wedge between us and I almost did lose him, I'm done keeping him at arm's length.

"Elle, you know I love you."

"I know you do."

He slides closer, taking the blanket from my lap and placing his hand on the side of my face, his thumb running along my cheek. "There's no turning back," he whispers, his lips growing closer.

"I know."

"As much as I want to promise if we don't work out, I'll still be your best friend, I can no longer guarantee that."

I nod. "I know."

"Are you sure?"

"Coop?"

He doesn't say anything but waits for me to speak again.

"Kiss me."

That panty-melting smile with both dimples transforms his face. "You don't have to tell me twice."

Inch by inch, breath by breath, second by second, he moves closer until his lips are on mine. Tentative at first, as if he's dipping his toes in a pool to feel the temperature.

All the anxiety that had been racing through my veins disappeared. All the worries that it would feel like I was kissing a brother vanished. All the nerves that he wouldn't want me are burned away in the fire. From the briefest of touches, it's there, the electricity we've been denying for years.

"Fuck, Elle." He says my name like a prayer as his hand slides to the back of my head, tilting it how he wants and diving in for a deeper kiss.

I open my mouth for him, and he slides his tongue in, exploring. When our tongues glide together, the best sound erupts from his throat as his hand tightens on my neck and his lips press firmer.

I cling to his arms, never wanting him to leave me, then I slide down the couch as he spreads my legs with his thigh. The yoga pants I'm wearing do nothing to block the feeling of his large bulge against my core. Our lips turn frantic, and I can't get close enough to him, my hands roaming up under the hem of his shirt.

He takes it by the collar and pulls it over his head, throwing it to the side.

I've seen Cooper's stomach plenty of times. Hell, the world has seen his stomach, but I allow the tips of my fingers to ghost down the dips and valleys of his abs. "God, you are…"

His head falls to the crook of my neck, sprinkling teasing kisses along my jaw and neck. "It's always been you, Elle. I've never wanted anyone the way I want you."

His breath causes a shiver to run up my spine.

"Damn, you feel so good over me," I say as his hands slip under my sweater, crawling up my belly. I arch my back off the couch in anticipation of him palming my breast, but instead, he runs his finger under the wire of my bra.

"I feel like a fucking teenage boy with how bad I want to touch your tits."

He reaches behind me with one hand, and I lift for him to unclasp my bra, loosening it around my chest. He lifts the sweater to my neck, nudging my bra out of the way, and takes my nipple into his mouth. Electric currents course through my body.

"Coop," I say, hurriedly stripping off my shirt and bra so he can touch, suck, lick, or do whatever he wants to do to my breasts.

He helps me, then stares at my naked chest. "I'll never have enough of these."

With one hand, he runs his finger and thumb along my nipple as his mouth licks and sucks my other breast. My legs widen, the ache of needing him inside me almost too much to bear.

"I'm not sure how long I can hold on, so…" He wiggles down my body, taking my leggings with him. Off the couch, he stands to remove my socks and leggings.

I take the opportunity to unbutton and unzip his jeans, leaving him in his boxer briefs. His hand cradles my head as I palm his erection through the thin fabric, staring up at him.

"That photo shoot was so hard. I was so hard," he confesses, and I laugh.

"Arousal is easier for girls to hide."

"I almost went back to your dressing room and fucked you senseless."

I give him a mock stern look. "Bradley wouldn't have liked that."

He dips so his forehead rests on mine, and I slide my hands up his thighs and under the edge of his underwear.

"Never say his name again, especially when your hand is on my dick."

I giggle. "Deal."

I fist him with one hand, pulling the elastic waist down with the other until it falls to his ankles. His head falls back, and he sighs as I pump him in my hand. There's something powerful about having his orgasm in my hands. This heart-throb of a man who women dream of is standing naked in front of me.

"You keep that up, and I'm gonna come."

I lean forward and lick his length from bottom to top before sucking on the tip of his dick.

He pulls his hips back so I can't reach him. "I'm definitely gonna come if you do that." He falls to his knees, denying me, and widens my legs with his hands on my inner thighs. "This is where I was headed before you interrupted me." He runs one knuckle over the wet silk of my black thong. "Damn, Elle, just when I think I can't get any harder."

His finger dips under the elastic and runs down my core, and my breath lodges in my throat. I grab his wrist to stop him from getting me off too soon. He chuckles and thrusts a finger inside me while his thumb plays with my clit in a torturous circular motion. I ride out the pleasure, and his other hand molds to my tit, grabbing it in a forceful manner and pinching my nipple. I rock against his hand, my fight to hold off dying as I ride out my orgasm.

"Beautiful." He sounds mesmerized. Cooper gets up and kisses my lips. "Just like I always imagined when I jacked off."

He reaches under my ass, picks me up with what seems like little effort, and his lips find mine again. Our kiss is still as needy and frantic as he walks us to the bedroom. Gently setting me on the bed, he stares down at me. No one has ever made me feel so wanton with just a look.

His dark eyes travel down my body and back up, lids

heavy. "You're so fucking hot. I can't believe how lucky I am to have you be mine."

He tears my thong from me and climbs onto the bed, over top of me. The tip of his cock hovers at my opening, pushing in a bit.

"Ah." I rise up on the bed a little. "Condom?"

"And that's why you're the doctor and I'm the football player." He crawls off me, then stills. "I don't have one."

Disappointment seeps into my pores. We've gotten this far. I mean, I've been tested and I'm sure he has, but I'm not on birth control, and I've seen how ineffective the pull-out method is. "Wait. They purposely put us up here alone, expecting us to work it out. I'm sure they were smart enough to leave condoms."

He nods. "You check that nightstand, and I'll check this one."

"Voilà!" I pull a box out with relief. "They're even ribbed for my pleasure. Thank you, Bryce and Adeline."

I toss it to him, and he rips the box open immediately, then tears a foil packet off a line of them. He's so fast and so skilled it's slightly unnerving. I've never really asked Cooper how many partners he's had over the years, but at the moment, I don't care. I lie down under him, needing to feel the fullness of him inside me.

He comes over to me with that damn smile—the one I never want to live without. "Where were we?"

The thick tip of him pushes into me, inch by inch.

"Right there," I say, barely able to breathe and feeling so full.

Cooper slowly withdraws, then sinks into me all over again, this time deeper. "I like here better." Then he lowers himself and nuzzles my face with his nose. "I've waited almost ten years for this moment, Elle, and it's a thousand times better than I ever thought it could be."

I grab his strong biceps. "Same."

He hovers over me, staring at me as though he can't believe we're doing this, but there's also love in his eyes. All the love and respect we have for one another that we've built between us through the years.

He rocks in and out of me, and my orgasm builds until I'm moaning. He falls with his arms on either side of my head, his lips finding mine. We kiss at a hurried pace, and he thrusts faster. I clench to keep my orgasm at bay, but Cooper has no plans on letting me achieve that goal.

"I'm never gonna get enough of you," he says.

"I'm right there with you."

"Fall apart for me. I want to see you come over and over again."

This time when he pulls out, he slams back inside me, and I groan with pleasure. I'm not sure where Cooper got all his moves, but he's already mastered me, and it's only our first time. I can't imagine what the future will bring.

His hand dips, and he plays with my clit, causing any control I had over my orgasm to crumble. The smirk on his lips says he knows he's playing dirty.

"God, Coop, I'm gonna come." The feeling is too intense not to give into it, and I succumb to the pleasure.

He drills in and out of me while his fingers circle my clit, and I come apart, screaming his name until I'm a sweaty mess on the bed.

"I'll never get enough of this," he whispers, pumping into me a few more times before a strangled cry escapes him with a string of incoherent words.

He falls on me, and I hold his sweaty body to mine, gripping him tightly as if he might disappear.

"I always knew we'd be good together, but shit…" he says.

"Yeah." That's all I manage to say because that was the best sex of my life.

I keep that to myself because I don't need to boost his ego too much after our first time.

He heads to the bathroom, and I slide under the covers. It doesn't take him long before he joins me, pulling me into his body.

"I love you," he whispers before kissing under my earlobe.

"I love you." I snuggle as close as I can, pulling his arms around me tighter.

There's no going back—thank God.

CHAPTER 18

COOPER

Waking up with Ellery in my arms gives me a feeling I can't explain—peace and contentment, followed by a flash of fear. I worry that I might be dreaming. Did I get a concussion in a game, or am I knocked out and this is all some dream?

She moves in my arms, but I slide out from holding her. She rolls over to her stomach and puts her arms under her pillow, her favorite sleeping position.

I dig through my bag and put on my lounge pants and a T-shirt before heading into the kitchen. The crew did good—the fridge is completely stocked for breakfast. I start the coffee, and while that's brewing, I crack some eggs to make us an omelet, cut up some fruit, and even make a small stack of pancakes.

"Am I in some rom-com movie?" Ellery walks in wrapped in a blanket, and suddenly breakfast doesn't look as appealing anymore.

"Are you naked under there?" I point at her with the spatula.

She nods.

"Fuck me, Elle."

She walks over and cuddles up to me. "Whenever you want." Her eyes sparkle, and I wind my arm around her. "It all smells so good."

"Have a seat. It's almost done." I kiss her temple.

But she doesn't move. "I don't really want to leave you. Our first morning together and you're not in bed when I wake up."

"Sorry, but I knew you'd be hungry since we didn't eat last night."

She nods. "You know me well."

We ended up having sex three more times last night, and after all the years we've known each other, I discovered something new—my favorite position so far is when she rides me.

I pick up a blueberry, putting it in front of her mouth. She opens it and takes it.

"I think we might be the stupidest couple ever," I say, turning off the burner and grabbing the plate of pancakes.

She walks in front of me to the table, then sits in the chair that faces the back of the cabin. Snow came down last night since we're so far north. Not that snow is unheard of in October in the Midwest.

"Why are you calling me stupid?" She plates her breakfast while her bare leg sneaks out of the comforter, teasing me.

"Because we waited so long for this." I catch her eye. "I'm so happy."

A slow smile spreads across her face, getting wider the longer our gazes lock. "Me too."

"Good." I lean forward and kiss her. "I'm half-tempted to make you sit on my lap so I can feed you."

"No way, we're not going to be one of *those* couples." She laughs.

This was something I worried about whenever I pictured us getting together. I knew I'd want to scream it from the rooftops and always be touching her, but she's weird about public affection. This is a lot of change, and I think I might have to ease her into it.

"What do you want to do today?" I ask, changing the subject because there's no way we're getting into a disagreement on day one. "I googled the small town near here, and they have some shopping event going on in their downtown."

"You wanna shop?" She forks a bite of pancake and eats it.

"Well, there isn't a ton to do, honestly. I can't ski unless I want Coach Stone to kick my ass on the off chance I get hurt."

"Hey, I have no problem shopping." She chuckles and finishes eating.

"I also need to know what day off you have next week."

Her head tilts. "Why?"

"I want to take you on a real date."

"Oh." Her anxiety is visible in the way her eyes shift away from mine. "What about photographers and stuff?"

"You've been photographed with me plenty of times."

She gives me a "duh" look. "This is different. We're together now."

Maybe I was wrong and she's down with some PDA now.

"People are going to find out. Well, the people who care. There are plenty who don't give a shit who I date." I eat my omelet, snagging a raspberry from the plate of fruit. "I'm ready for them to know you aren't just my best friend anymore. I want to scream into every microphone in the world about how I scored the most amazing woman."

I hold out my hand, and she comes over and sits in my lap. "I'm not sure I'm ready for the public criticism. Remember Adeline?"

"You know where you stand in my life. Don't listen to them."

She laughs. "You're delusional sometimes."

"No, I'm not. People will be happy for us."

Her eyebrows lift. "Well." She picks up a raspberry and

lets the blanket fall open, placing it on her nipple. "We'll have to agree to disagree for now because a raspberry has gone astray."

I bend down and take the raspberry into my mouth, licking her nipple as I do. Standing, I hoist her up firefighter-style and leave the room.

"Where are we going?"

"Back to bed."

"I'm still hungry. You know I'm not one of those salad girls." She hits my ass before sliding her hands down my pajama pants.

"I'll feed you." I drop her on the mattress, and she's now at eye level with my dick.

"Oh, he'll do." She pulls down my pajama pants and takes my dick into my hands, licking her lips.

It's another two hours before we finally get in the shower and get ready to go out.

Turns out our friends just parked the minivan at the neighbors'. I went outside to see how cold it was before we tried to find an Uber or a cab and spotted it. The owner returned it to us in exchange for me signing a few things. Turns out he used to live outside of Chicago, so he's a Grizzlies fan. That's probably why he agreed to keep the van in his driveway for the duration of the weekend in the first place.

We're on the road, looking like a married couple without their kids in tow and on the way to the Fall Fest when Ellery's phone pings.

"Who is it?" I ask when she slides her hand out of mine to pull the phone out of her purse.

"Bryce."

"Let's play with them a little," I say.

"Yeah, okay. I'm going to tell her that you left last night." She types it out, and her phone pings like crazy. "She's sending those rapid-fire texts where she doesn't finish the sentence. She starts by saying, 'What?' then, 'No way.' Then, 'I thought my plan was brilliant.'"

"Tell her you've been crying all night. Our fight got worse, and I stormed out. That I'm probably back in Chicago already and you're stranded."

"Oh, that's evil. They'll know you're not there." She bites her inner cheek like she does when she's deciding if she really wants to do something.

"They let us come up here without knowing we'd end up where we are. They deserve a little of their own medicine."

She nods and her fingers fly across the screen. I pull into the town area, which looks as though it could be a movie set.

"Oh, this is so cute." She pockets her phone and opens the door.

We're not even thirty seconds away from the van when her phone pings and mine does too.

She pulls hers out, and I grab it from her, turning it off before I turn off mine. "No more interruptions."

"Work?"

I shake my head. "Work doesn't need you. You're off."

"Okay. I'm going to have major anxiety about this, but maybe in the end it will feel freeing." She tucks the phone into her purse, and we walk down the street.

We go into every shop, from the candy and chocolate store to a pottery place. We eat lunch at a local brewery, and the entire time, I can't keep my hands off of her. And she doesn't seem to mind, kissing me in public as if it's no big thing. Maybe I was worried for no reason.

After lunch, we drop the bags in the van and take a walk through the park.

"I was thinking... when we get back, whose place are we going to stay at?" I link our fingers together.

"What do you mean?" She knocks her shoulder with mine.

"Do you think I'm going to be able to not sleep in the same bed as you now?"

She looks at me a little quizzically. "It's only been one night."

I stop us from walking any farther. "So, you're saying you want to sleep away from me?"

She lets me hold her close, my hands linked behind her back, her hands on my chest. "I'm saying I'm on call a lot, and you're in the middle of your season."

"Exactly, so we need to make the most of the time we have together. I vote for The Den. My place is bigger."

"Barely." She scoffs.

"Since I own the building, you could just give up your place, save your money, and we can move in together."

Her eyes bore into me for a moment. "You're serious?"

I lock my arms tighter around her. "Don't you think we've spent enough time apart?" I kiss her to convince her, and she doesn't object when I slide my tongue into her mouth. "So?"

"So, you're not getting an answer, and as great of a kisser as you are, it won't influence me." She squirms out of my hold. "Give it time. It's been one night, Coop."

I sigh. "I just hate the thought of driving back tomorrow and saying goodbye to you. Now that I have you, I don't want to let you go."

She laughs. "I get that, but I'm not going anywhere." She wraps her arms around my neck. "I want to be wherever you are. And I'm so happy we've finally gotten here. But we *just* got here, Cooper. Give it some time. You might even get annoyed with me."

"Never," I say, knowing I never got annoyed when she was my friend and vice versa. "You know me…"

"Yes, you're impatient and want what you want now. I know what I'm getting myself into." She smiles. "Enough touristy stuff. All this talk about going back tomorrow makes me want to make the most of the time we have here. There are no distractions here. Nothing to pull us away from one another, so take me back to the cabin and show me exactly what I've been missing all these years with only being your friend." She licks her lips.

"Let's go." I pick her up and walk back to the minivan.

"Coop, put me down," she says as she laughs.

"Not on your life."

I get her in the minivan and drive faster than I should back to the cabin. We use the code to get in, and we're stripping each other's clothes off before the door is even shut. Getting tangled in her jeans, she falls to the floor laughing, and I squat next to her to help, but she grabs me and pulls me down, placing her lips on mine.

Our kiss only stays PG for so long before we're in R-rated territory, continuing to undress each other on the floor.

"Fuck, condom," I mumble, climbing off her.

"I'll go with you."

"Stay put."

"I'm not a dog," she says.

I grab the box of condoms and drop them on the coffee table in the family room, then slide one on, meeting her back on the floor. I thrust inside her, and we each moan at the sensation.

"You feel so good." She holds me close.

I lift one of her legs over my shoulder to get as deep as I can. "How about now?"

"I have no words." She grabs my neck, smashing her lips to mine.

After we finish, I start the fire, lay blankets in front of it, and ask her to join me. We lie on the floor, caressing one another and kissing while we talk about nothing and everything all at once.

An hour later, she climbs on top of me, and I can't help but grin. The glow of the fire really brings out her beauty.

"I don't want you to think that I don't want this," she says. "I'm one hundred percent in this. I promise you that. I just don't want to go full steam ahead. Part of the fun is dating. I get that we've known each other a long time, but…"

"You want to be wooed?"

Her cheeks blush, and she shrugs. "Maybe a little bit."

I raise up and kiss her. "Consider it done."

CHAPTER 19

ELLERY

I didn't prepare myself for Cooper Rice's wooing.

The next morning, there's another breakfast waiting for me, this time a huge spread since there's so much food that will go bad in the fridge since it's our last day here.

I grab my phone halfway through our meal and realize that I never turned it back on after our day trip yesterday. "Shit."

Cooper leans back in his seat, sipping his coffee.

"Well, if we thought we had until we got back for people to figure it out, we're wrong. Bryce sent this over to me." Something in my gut told me those ladies on the park bench were staring at us a little hard, but I thought they were moms, and Cooper had a hat on.

I turn the phone for him to see the picture of us kissing on the path, another one of him carrying me to the car, me laughing, and a third of us walking around packages after shopping downtown. The headline under the kissing picture reads, "Looks like Cooper Rice finally found love with his best friend."

He stands, kisses me, and goes into the kitchen. Refilling his cup, he doesn't say a word.

"You have nothing to say?"

He shrugs. "People were going to find out one way or another. Now it's done with."

"Bryce says people are speculating whether this is going to be good or bad for you. That maybe I'm a distraction you don't need. And she said some people aren't being kind about the fact that I was with Bradley first and now you."

My stomach drops. Sure, I've been photographed with Cooper, and we've always maintained that we're best friends, so there was never any judgment except for the people who said a man and woman can't be just friends. Now, I've opened myself to ridicule online. I pray I don't affect his game, otherwise it will only get worse.

"They don't have to worry about my game, that's my responsibility. All I care about is you and me." He comes back over, kissing me before he sits down at the table.

"Coop."

He's already shaking his head. "Nope. We don't care about those people. They sure as hell don't care about us, they don't even really know us. The football fans only care if I'm performing well enough for their fantasy football league, and the single women think they should be the ones on my arm. I learned a long time ago to not give a shit. None of them can come on that field and do what I do." I bite my lip, causing him to stop and scrunch his eyebrows at me. "What?"

I stand and walk over to straddle him on his chair. "You're really sexy when you're being all 'I'll tell you how it is.'"

He grins, and his hands slide under my shirt and he pulls me closer to him. "Should we talk about my views on politics?"

I laugh. "No. Definitely not. I just like it that way you're all like, 'This is my life and they can all be damned.'"

"It's true." He stares into my eyes so hard I grow a little uncomfortable with the intensity of the intimacy, but my gaze doesn't leave his. "It's taken us so long to get here, I'm not going to let anyone tell us it's bad. And they'll see next game day that I'm still the same quarterback they had before his gorgeous best friend snapped him up."

I wrap my arms around him, nuzzling into his arms. I'm sore from how many times we've had sex, though I still ache to have him inside of me. Will that ever go away?

His hands run down my back. "I won't allow anyone or anything to come between us. I promise, Elle." He kisses the top of my head.

"I just wish we could stay here forever."

"Me too."

We stay like that for a while, but as soon as we get back to Chicago, I know our bubble is going to burst. I'm scared it could be like a tsunami, and it won't matter how tight Cooper's hand is in mine, they'll slip apart.

Cooper rings the downstairs buzzer of my apartment building even though he has a key.

"Who is it?" I pretend to not know.

"I'm here to pick up Ellery?" he asks.

I chuckle. "I'll be right down."

He hits the buzzer again.

"Yes?" I answer.

"You're not going to invite me up?"

"This is our first date, and I'm sorry, but I don't let strange men up to my apartment on the first date."

He laughs. "Fair enough."

I grab my clutch and look at my dress. It's a shorter green one that cinches at the waist and only goes out a little bit over the legs. Walking down the stairs, my stomach fills with butterflies because I have no idea what he has planned for us tonight.

I purposely didn't let him spend the night Sunday or

Monday, and I didn't stay at his place either. I hope I can kiss him goodbye on the porch, but my willpower has to be strong.

I open up the door to my apartment building and find him standing by a car with a driver. Any willpower I had flies down the street with the fallen leaves from the trees. Cooper Rice cleans up well, and I've known that as long as I've known him, but there's something different now that he's mine.

He approaches me dressed in a suit, with a bouquet of flowers in hand. "You look stunning," he whispers, leaning in and kissing me on the cheek. Very first-date behavior.

"Thank you." I smell the flowers. "And for these, too."

"It's funny that I know so much about you, but I don't know what your favorite flower is."

"Honestly? I don't have one, so this assortment is beautiful. Should I run it up, quick?" I ask.

"Sure, I'll help you." He places his hand on the small of my back and gestures with his other hand for me to lead the way.

I shake my head. "I think they'll survive."

"I'm not getting in that apartment tonight, am I?" he whispers.

A few guys walk by and stop, seeing Cooper, but they only nod and continue walking. Cooper should go give them an autograph and a selfie for not interrupting our date.

"I'm not sure yet."

I walk to the car, and he opens up the door for me. Sliding in, the driver introduces himself as Seth and then puts up the barrier as soon as Cooper climbs in next to me. Obviously, there were some conversations about what Cooper wanted before I was picked up.

"It's taking everything in me not to call off this dinner and take you back to my place," he says, his hand sliding to the back of my neck and drawing me in for a kiss.

His lips move slow and tender, his tongue gliding along the seam of my lips, asking permission. I open for him, and his tongue slides along mine in the perfect rhythm we mastered this past weekend. This is the man I'll kiss for the rest of my life, I just know it, and I'm thankful he's so damn good.

I lose myself in his gentle caresses, sweet kisses, and soft demeanor. He's right, let's just go to one of our places. I don't need to be wooed. The man has done so many nice things for me my entire life, I know what he's capable of. But the other side of me says, this will be fun, it's like we're doing everything backward. We're in love and just now getting to the dating part.

I protest with a groan when he closes the kiss, leaving me with one last touch of his lips.

"No questions, yet?"

"I'm wondering where you're taking me." I look out the window. The stop-and-go traffic is already telling me we haven't left the downtown area.

"That I cannot answer. But..."

"Are you going to answer anything?"

He shakes his head. I knew he'd be like that.

"Fine then." I roll my eyes.

We each talk about how our day was, he was off, and I worked the early shift today. I don't remind him that I'm on early tomorrow too, so there won't be any sex fest going on tonight.

The car pulls off the curb, and I wait impatiently to see what Cooper has planned.

In all the years I've known him, we've never really discussed our previous relationships. He never came to me for advice on what to do if he was taking a girl out on a date or divulged much of anything that happened on his dates. I never wanted to say a word about the dates I went on because it felt weird. I'm guessing that's because of all the feelings we harbored for one another that we pretended were in the realm of friendship.

I reach over and squeeze his hand, and he flips it over and links our fingers. We look at one another, our eyes catching, both smiling. I'm a lucky, lucky woman. Cooper couldn't be more perfect for me.

We're in traffic for the entire ride, and when we stop, I see a huge theater sign hanging from the building.

"Really?" I ask, staring up at the marquee.

"Really."

"But—" I want to protest because Cooper has always said he finds plays and musicals boring.

"It won't be boring with you up in the private box with me."

"Private box?" I'm smiling so wide my face feels like it might crack.

He laughs. "Only the best for you."

My cheeks flush, and he exits the car, keeping the door open and holding out his hand for me.

Once I step out onto the sidewalk, a flash goes off, blinding me. Cooper pulls me into his body. "There's only two photographers here, and they're probably looking for someone with a bigger name than me," he whispers into my ear.

"Cooper!" one of them yells as we make our way to the theater entrance.

Cooper nods in acknowledgment, opens the door, and we both file into the theater. He shows our tickets, and we're escorted up to our seats. We're some of the last to arrive, the rest of the theater already filled in with people chatting before the show starts. I'm betting he planned that on purpose.

There are only two seats, and we're in the very first box. It's a breathtaking view.

"Cooper." I sigh thinking about what he must have paid for these tickets.

He sits down in the seat the furthest from the stage, allowing me to have the closest seat.

A girl could get addicted to this kind of behavior.

I lean over and kiss him as a thank you, but he deepens the kiss, moaning into my mouth. He pulls me as close as he can while sitting in two separate chairs. This man drives me wild. I could straddle him in a second or fall to my knees for him.

Instead, I lean back, catching my breath. "Be good, Mr. Rice."

"Or what?" he whispers. "You've already warned me I won't get to sleep with you tonight. I should've copped a feel earlier."

I laugh, and he smiles. He leans in millimeters from my ear, whispering, "I'm not joking. Do you have any idea what it's like to walk around with a hard-on all day? Anytime I remember us in bed together, how perfect your tits look, bare and ready for me… your soaked silk thongs, my dick springs up to attention."

Oh fuck, he's going to make me give in on the whole "no sleepover" thing if he keeps talking like that.

I'm saved from having to respond as the lights dim and the curtains open.

Cooper slides his chair as close to me as he can, wrapping his arm around the back of my chair. His fingers tease the curve of my neck, gliding over my skin ever so gently.

If I make it through the entire show without jumping his bones, I deserve a medal.

CHAPTER 20

COOPER

I kiss her one more time, and her lips are just as eager as mine. We've been making out in my apartment for over twenty minutes now.

"Coop." She pushes me back with her hands. "We're already late."

"It's two flights of stairs. I'm not sure why we said yes to begin with." My head falls into the crook of her neck, nibbling on her earlobe.

"They're our friends, and they invited us over. Bryce says you're keeping me all to yourself since we became a couple." She wiggles, and I grind my pelvis against hers. She rocks against my hard length.

"Who is tempting who now?" I allow her to grind against me as I push into her. "A quickie. I can't go up there like this. It won't go down until we fuck."

"First of all, we don't have time to satisfy you, otherwise we would already be naked. Second, you act like it's been a month when it's been about ten hours."

"Yes, this morning. That's not cutting it anymore. I need you more than that."

She slides out from under me. "Hence the reason I had to

put our sleepovers on a schedule. Dr. Murphy found me sleeping at the desk the other day."

Shit, I definitely don't want to affect her career. "I'm sorry."

She gets up and straightens her sweater, putting on her shoes. "It's not the first time, and it won't be the last time someone falls asleep on shift, but I'd rather have the excuse that I worked a double rather than I fucked my boyfriend so many times last night you should be surprised I can even walk." She gives me a cheeky grin.

"I don't know if I respect that last excuse." I pull her back toward me. "Just tell me no next time, and I'll go into the bathroom and see to it myself."

"That's the problem, I want it just as much as you." She turns her head and kisses my lips. I don't even try to deepen it, rather I release her so we can head to Miles and Bryce's.

I push my feet into my slides and swipe my keys off the counter. Opening the door for her, she gets out first and starts ascending the stairs, and I quickly catch up.

"I might have to meet Dr. Murphy in a dark alley one of these days."

She hooks her arm with mine, nuzzling into me because the stairway is chilled from the cold front coming in tonight. The decent Chicago weather is about to be over for at least the next five months. "No, you don't. He's harmless, just doesn't want me to get special treatment because of my father."

"The man deserves to get his ass kicked."

"Thanks for wanting to beat him up for me. It's so very high school jock mentality of you, but it turns me on, so don't do it in real life, but you can keep saying you want to." She laughs, and I press the doorbell and take her in my arms.

"Are you sure you wouldn't get all hot if you saw me punch him?"

"I'm pretty sure."

The door opens, and Bryce stands there, not saying a word. "So weird," she finally says.

"What is?" Ellery asks.

"The two of you touching like that." She wags her finger between us.

"Would you rather just see us fuck and get the awkwardness out of the way?" I arch an eyebrow.

"Are you asking my wife for a threesome?" Miles comes over, shaking my hand and then hugging Ellery. "Nice to see the two of you made it out of the cabin alive."

"And I've yet to give you shit for turning off your phones like that." Bryce's head tilts, and she gives us both a stern look.

Ellery and I head inside the apartment.

"Were you really worried?" Ellery asks.

They both laugh. "No, we knew it was brewing and ready to be poured out. You guys love each other as people, best friends, and lovers. He wouldn't leave you. I'm not stupid." Bryce shakes her head. "Come on. Damon and Adeline are on their way. Clover had a little meltdown downstairs over dinner, so they're dealing with that."

We walk into the apartment, which is the same setup as mine, except Miles is on the top floor. When I bought this building, all three units were newly renovated, and they all had access to the rooftop to watch the Colts games. Since baseball is my second love, I knew it would be a good investment. Now that I have Ellery and my thoughts keep going to our future, I know this isn't a forever place—there's no room for a family here.

A knock on the door says Damon and Adeline are here, and I swipe a chip with salsa from the table since I'm hungry. One good thing about Bryce coming into Miles's life is we don't get stuck eating rice cakes and green smoothies anymore when he invites us over.

Miles gets the door while Bryce keeps staring at me and Ellery like we're an exhibit at the zoo.

"What?" Ellery asks, snagging a carrot stick with hummus.

"It's just so… I mean, I've waited so long for it to happen." Her eyes look like those cartoon characters with the two giant hearts pulsing.

"That makes three of us," I say.

"We're still just Ellery and Cooper," Elle says, then smiles at seeing Clover walk into the room. "Ah… look at you, big girl." She squats, and Clover walks unsteadily right into her arms.

Ellery picks her up and holds her to her chest, praising her for her walking.

It feels like a flash of our future—Elle with our own daughter one day in this same position. God, she'll be a great mom. Her bedside manner with her patients is always loving, caring, and supportive.

"She's getting way too big," she says to Adeline, letting Clover down since she squirms in her arms.

"And nosy and defiant and… bratty." She whispers the last word.

"Sounds like Damon." Bryce laughs.

"She threw a fit today because she didn't want to leave the playground at the park. Like threw herself on the ground and wailed. Then she threw sand at Damon when he went to get her."

All of our mouths drop open. Damon's definitely the more relaxed parent when it comes to discipline. He thought it was funny when Clover started throwing food, but Adeline put a stop to it.

"I almost lost it in front of a bunch of parents," Adeline says.

"What did you do?" I ask.

Adeline laughs, handing Clover her snack cup.

Damon looks at Adeline like, "Shut the hell up, it wasn't funny." "I went over, picked her up so her back was facing me, and she couldn't get sand in my eye. I then took her to an empty bench, sat her down, and scolded her."

"And what did she do?" Miles asks.

"She rolled on her stomach, got off the bench, and went back to the park," he grumbles.

"You've babied her. She doesn't take you seriously when you try to discipline her." Adeline shakes her head.

"What can I say, I'm weak for the women I love." Damon smiles wide.

We all say, "Ahh…" in unison.

"Unless you want a child we're always being dragged into school about, I suggest we double down on her. I can't imagine what she'll be like when she's two." Clover walks over to Adeline and takes her sippy cup from her, handing back the snack cup.

"Yeah, yeah. I know."

Ellery walks over to me behind the breakfast bar, and I wrap my arm around her, pulling her close as she eats more appetizers. I catch Adeline watching us with a smile on her face. Apparently, we're the new attraction. She catches me watching her, and her smile grows bigger before turning away.

"PDA alert!" Damon shouts. "Holy hell, that's about fucking time."

"Damon," Adeline scolds. "If her first coherent word is the f-word, I'm writing down how it's all your fault in the baby book."

He holds up his hands and turns back to me and Ellery. "So, does it feel different?"

Ellery looks up at me, and we both shrug. "No," I answer for us.

"It wasn't weird when you saw each other naked?" He keeps prying.

"We've seen each other by accident before," Ellery says, like it wasn't a big deal to be totally naked with her at the cabin.

For me, it was at first. To unapologetically be allowed to just stare at her perfect body after imagining it for so many years. It wasn't weird, it was more like wanting something for so long that when you finally get it, you're afraid to ruin it.

"Okay, but it had to be weird watching his dick go into you."

"Damon!" we all shout at once.

"Fine, well, you look good together, but we all knew that years ago. Congratulations on finally listening to what people have been telling you forever."

"I should get some drinks so we can all celebrate." Miles walks over to the fridge.

"That's not necessary. Everyone is making too big a deal of this," Ellery says.

I say, "Hell yeah, let's celebrate. I finally have my girl."

"Bryce and I have news to share, too," Miles says.

"So do Adeline and I," Damon says.

All six of us look at one another, trying to decipher each other's news. Shit, is one of them thinking of retiring after this year? Hell, Damon doesn't have to work, and I know he hates not being with Clover as much as he'd like during the season.

"Let me pour the champagne, and then we'll all go around." Miles grabs a bottle from the fridge, and Bryce goes over to help grab the glasses.

Damon feeds Clover some of the snacks in small pieces, and she smiles up at him. Damn, it's endearing as hell watching the two of them. Makes me want one of my own now that I have Ellery.

"I can't wait," I whisper in Ellery's ear.

Her forehead creases. "For?"

I nod in Clover's direction. "One of those. Half you and me."

Her head whips in my direction, and she's staring at me with a "What the fuck?" expression.

"I'm not ready," she says with a finality that scares me for a moment. But we're only in our early thirties, we have a year or two before we should really look into it. It sours me a little bit that she was against it so fast. I hope that's not a trend.

"Here you go." Miles and Bryce pass out the champagne glasses.

We all hold them up.

"First off, I want to say congratulations, you two." Bryce smiles over at us. "I speak for all of us when I say I hope you are as happy as we are. You might have taken the longer road to get where you are, but it's the present and the future that matter the most, not the past." She raises her glass, and we all clink and take a sip.

"Me," Clover says, and we all know what she means. She raises her sippy cup, and we all clink it, making her show off those four bottom teeth in her smile.

Damon clears his throat. "It's been a hard decision to make, and we hate to tell you this, but we're moving out of The Den." He looks distraught. "With Clover, we just can't do it anymore. She needs a yard, and we need a bigger space."

"Her toys are swallowing us whole," Adeline jokes, and we all laugh.

"Did you already find a place?" I ask.

"We think so, but we're waiting to see if the offer goes through. I'll pay my year here too."

We'll figure something out, I'm not worried about it.

"Congratulations! I want to see pictures," Ellery says to Adeline.

We all clink again, including Clover. She laughs at us.

"That leaves us, babe," Miles says to Bryce.

I hope they're not leaving, too.

"You do it," Bryce says.

"We're pregnant," Miles announces with a wide grin.

"Shit, there's a baby in your stomach?" Damon looks at Miles.

"You know what I meant," Miles says with a roll of his eyes and tips his glass toward Bryce. "Bryce is pregnant."

The girls screech and wrap each other up in a hug. Bryce starts telling them the whole story, while I hold my hand out to shake Miles' and congratulate him on starting a family.

I can't help but feel a little left behind.

I watch all the women and Clover huddle by the couches, laughing and sharing what's been going on in their lives. Maybe Ellery just needs time to get used to us being a couple. There's still so much we haven't endured while being friends that we'll embark on as a couple. The last thing I want to do is scare her off.

CHAPTER 21

ELLERY

"I can't believe you're pregnant," Adeline says to Bryce.

"I know. It's crazy, when we said we were done with birth control, I thought it would take a while, but bam, one month and I'm pregnant." She's smiling, one I've never seen on her before. She's beaming now that I look closely at her.

"And he or she won't be far off in age from Clover. If Damon has his way, I'll bet he's gonna try to knock me up tonight just so we can have babies close to the same age." Adeline laughs. "He likes the idea of all of us living on the same block for the rest of our lives and our kids growing up together."

I choke on the last sip of my champagne, and they both look at me.

"I'm sorry, we didn't mean to take over your night of celebration." Bryce bites her lip like she's worried.

"There's nothing to celebrate. Yes, Cooper and I are a couple, but it doesn't change anything."

"You're kidding. It changes everything." Bryce's mouth falls open. "How could you say that? Aren't you excited?" Her brows draw down.

"Yes, and I'm happy. *We're* happy."

How do I tell my friends, who convinced me to make it happen and are invested in my relationship, that it's all happening too fast? I haven't had a chance to just take a breath. I've either seen Cooper or talked to him numerous times per day, every day. He surprises me at work, he surprises me at my apartment, and he surprises me with plans when I'm exhausted after a shift. But I don't want to make him feel bad, and I really do want to spend time with him.

Bryce reaches over and touches my knee. "Elle?"

I shake my head and glance over at the guys who are involved in their own conversation and not paying us any attention. "No. I'm glad we crossed the line… it's just that we've gone from being best friends to dating for five years overnight."

Adeline leans back on the couch, giving me a look as if she feels bad for me. She was thrust into the same situation when she was pregnant and handled it fine, so I'm sure she doesn't understand where I'm coming from.

Clover climbs into her mom's lap and plays with her toy.

Do I want one of those? I think so. But I'm still making a name for myself at work.

"Probably because you've known one another for so long. Like there's no getting to know each other except in the bedroom," Adeline says, and that makes sense. "I mean, Damon and I got thrown into this, but we still had to get to know one another. Thankfully, it worked out, but in most cases, it doesn't."

"I'm sure there's a lot of friends to lovers who don't make it the long haul either," I say, and Bryce scoffs.

"Don't do this, Elle," she says, standing.

"What are you talking about?" I frown.

"Sabotage something good. Slow it down if you have to, but you'll regret it if you lose him."

What the fuck? Was I speaking a foreign language?

"Bryce?"

She sits down when I give her the look that we're not finished here. "I am not going to end this. I love him. I *am* happy. But I don't want to plan my entire future right now. I don't want to look at houses or think about having a baby. I want to know what it would've felt like ten years ago when I met Cooper. If we wouldn't have listened to all the bullshit about sex ruining our futures and our friendship, what would he have done to get me to like him? What would I have done? I don't want that to not be part of our story."

She stares at me. She's always a harsh critic and probably doesn't understand what I'm saying. "I'm sure Adeline didn't want to get to know Damon while six months pregnant. You're forgetting Elle, you did get to know him in small increments as you two became best friends. And that's what's going to make it last. Don't you see what a bonus that is and not a strike against you?"

I look behind me at the guys surrounding the breakfast bar, eating, laughing, and having fun. Cooper looks like there's nothing that could ruin his mood right now. He's high on life because of us. As if he can read me, he turns my way and winks. Those dimples are going to be the death of me.

"I do. But…" I shake my head, not wanting to get into it, especially with him only a few feet away. "Just forget it, I'm not explaining it right."

Bryce stands and goes to join the guys.

Adeline's hand falls to my leg. "I get it. I do. I wished I could turn back time so many times. That I would've played harder to get. If I did, would Damon have chased me?" She shrugs. "Doubtful, but I'll never really know. Then I realized it didn't matter. This little one brought us together, and that's all that matters. So, relax. All relationships go at different speeds. No one is saying you need to be engaged, looking at houses or wedding dresses. And Cooper loves you, so trust him with your worries."

I squeeze her hand on my leg. She doesn't know Cooper though. If I tell him I want to slow down, he'll be just like Bryce and think there's something wrong. This is something I have to get over myself so that I don't hurt him. And I will, I just need a little time.

Bryce comes back over, and Adeline shows us the pictures of the new house. It's beautiful, with a small yard in the back for Clover. It's not far from The Den but in a more family-friendly area of the city.

How can Damon take this all in stride? Up until two years ago, he was a womanizer, sleeping with women and never wanting a commitment. And now he's married with a kid, wanting another one, and buying a house in an area with zero nightlife. Surely, if Damon can go from one to sixty in such a short time, I can too.

"Hi, I'm Dr. Wallace," I say, sanitizing my hands and walking into the patient's room.

There's a man in there with a woman seated next to him on her phone. She tucks it away in her purse and gives me all her attention. "You're Cooper Rice's girlfriend," she says. "The quarterback for—"

"Yes, I am." I offer her a smile.

"I just saw you on my feed. You two make a cute couple."

"Thank you." I turn my attention to the patient. "What brings you in today, Mr. Hunt?"

"I hope your man plays a good game on Sunday. There's a lot of predictions out there that you could either make or break his game. It happens all the time, they get a girlfriend, and their game goes to shit."

I offer him a wane smile and push down my frustration.

"Well, I hope so too. So, Nurse Janet told me that you have some stomach pain. Can you tell me where?"

"Right here." He points to his lower right side. It's in the area of his appendix. "I remember this one guy, I don't even remember his name, but he was gonna be the next big player, his number had been called up like they say. Got himself a girl, and it all went to shit. I think he's third string somewhere now, signing one-year contracts."

"And how long have you had the pain?" I ask, not wanting to continue this line of conversation.

"About a week."

"I don't know how you girls do it. I could never date someone like that. All the competition for his attention. The out-of-town games. That man is gorgeous and could get anyone even if they didn't know who he was, which I'm sure they do."

I move over to the computer to pull up his file, trying not to engage.

"Can you give me a number one through ten for how intense the pain is?" I'm pretty sure I could give him a number. I've been doing this long enough to know that a man in pain wouldn't be sitting here gossiping about my relationship instead of complaining about how much pain he's in.

"An eight. It's gotten worse tonight," he says.

I type it in. "I'm going to send you down for a CT scan of the abdomen. It's late, so the results should come back within an hour or so. We'll go from there. I'll get your bloodwork going as well." I go to leave, but the wife stops me.

"You keep that man on a leash if you want him to stick around," she says, smiling like she's just delivering me good advice.

I manage a small smile and leave the room.

As I'm writing out the orders for his tests, Alice comes along one side of me with Hayes on the other.

"So?" they both say in unison.

I groan. "Not today, please."

"We've been waiting all week to work a shift with you. You have to fill us in," Alice practically whines.

"Is he good in bed? I bet he is," Hayes says. "Men with that kind of confidence always are."

I turn to one and then the other. "I have to work."

I would be talking to them about this, but after the Hunts' opinions, I'm not really in the mood.

"Well, I say it's about time. I love Cooper and I love you, so the two of you together is perfection." Alice beams, sipping the coffee she grabbed from the gourmet place down the block.

"Yeah, and I did not like that Bradley guy. At the flu drive, he was a complete douche." Hayes circles in his chair like he's a kid.

"Let me guess, Dr. Wallace, or should I say Mr. Quarterback's girl, is giving you the scoop." I turn to see Dr. Murphy holding a cup of gourmet coffee in his hand—from the same place that Alice got hers from.

My gaze whips over to Alice, and she stares at me for a moment before my attention drops to her cup, and she follows my vision. She gets a sheepish look on her face.

"I am Dr. Murphy, and I was putting orders in for Mr. Hunt in room fourteen." I finish typing and start to walk away.

Hayes continues to circle in his chair, getting Nurse Janet to give him a spin as she walks by.

Alice doesn't follow me, and I don't expect her to.

"I have a package!" Nurse Jennifer comes in the back from the intake desk. "It's for… Dr. Wallace, soon to be Dr. Rice." Her eyebrows waggle up and down.

I take the package out of her hands a little more aggressively than I should. "Sorry. And I'll never be Dr. Rice, I'm keeping my name." I start walking again, then turn back around. "And there's no wedding. We're dating, that's all!" I say loud enough for everyone to hear.

All eyes turn to me.

"We can all read, Dr. Wallace." Dr. Murphy turns around and heads down the hall.

I mangle the box open and find some chocolate from Cooper's favorite place. I'm not sure when he ordered it, but he gets the emergency room a box every year, so I can't fault him.

"This is why we love Cooper!" Hayes says, dropping his candy bar from the vending machine and diving into the box. "Bring on the peanut butter ones."

"Leave the marshmallow ones for me." Alice shoves Hayes out of the way.

"Jesus, you're all gonna end up being patients." Dr. Mendez comes over. "I love these chocolate balls." She holds one up, and none of them says anything because, hell, it's Dr. Mendez.

I smile and she walks away, then all three of us burst out laughing once the doors shut behind her.

Why does Cooper always have perfect timing? I'm upset because it's like I've gone from being a doctor to just a girlfriend overnight. Patients are only here to ask me about being his girlfriend, and then I get delivered a box of candy, and I'm laughing with my coworkers. Damn him.

CHAPTER 22
COOPER

"Can you keep your mind off her for the next few hours?" Damon smacks me on the back, laughing.

"Fuck off."

If I have to hear from one more person that my game is gonna go to shit because I'm in love, I'm gonna go ape shit. She's been my best friend for over ten years, and maybe what people don't understand is that I've been in love with her the entire time. She comes to all my home games and was by my side for the last two championships. So, everyone who thinks that I'm gonna choke or something can go to hell.

"Relax, I'm on your side." Damon suits up, glancing over at Miles.

I sit down on the bench, mindful of who's in the room. "It's just…" Fuck, I didn't want to talk to anyone about this. I'm sure I'm just paranoid of losing her now that I finally have her. "I think she's pulling away."

"What?" Damon scoffs. "No way."

I nod. "Every time I talk to her about our future and marriage or kids, she just clams up. She's put stipulations on when we can see one another, how many nights, and shit like that."

"But when you're together?" Miles asks.

"Lights out, man. She's all over me, I'm all over her. We can't get enough of one another."

"What else do you guys do when you're together?" Damon asks.

I take a second to think about it. "I took her to a play, and we went to dinner. It's only been a week, so other than that, it's just ordering food and watching movies or shows that don't get watched because we're all over one another."

"Look at it this way, you've had ten years of friend dates and getting to know another. You're in the sex-crazed part of the relationship now. Enjoy it because it ends," Miles says.

"Wait until your little one arrives," Damon chimes in, eyeing Miles.

"Enjoy the sex now, and from what I know of Ellery, which isn't as much as you and Bryce know, she likes things slow. Doesn't want to rush into anything." Miles is so perceptive of people.

"Yeah, she does." When she was deciding what to specialize in during medical school, she went from family to obstetrics to emergency. And when she got her apartment, she flip-flopped between two units, unable to make the decision because she's always worried about making a mistake. Amazing how someone can have a job where they have to be so decisive but not when it comes to her personal life. "Okay. I'll give it more time."

"You're the only man I know who would complain about too much pussy and not enough planning." Damon shakes his head and finishes getting dressed.

Coach Stone comes out of his office, huddles us together for a pep talk, and sends us out to the field, ready to win.

We run out, and Damon pisses off Coach Stone by jumping into the stands with Adeline and Clover, who is here today, along with Adeline's parents.

Bryce is waving to Miles, wearing her usual plethora of things with his number on them.

My gaze shifts to the only person I care about. Ellery smiles and gives me a wave as if she can keep what's between us hidden. I blow her a kiss, and her smile widens until her vision shifts to my side.

"Funny, if you would've just been honest with me, I never would've gone after her." Bradley stretches his arm across his chest. "And look at that smile now that she's all snug back in your number."

"I didn't know what I felt then," I say.

"Bullshit. But I'm glad you both opened up your eyes so you can stop screwing over others."

I laugh and rock my head back. "Are you suggesting that she hurt you?"

"Not her, but your stunt in the nightclub got me suspended for a game. What you're missing, Golden Boy, is that I'm not you. I never won the Player of the Year award, I didn't have a daddy who paved the road for me, and I don't have your record. So, me being suspended makes me look like I'm a problem. And teams don't like problems. All that bullshit because you guys were too afraid to lose each other may have cost me a position with another team."

"You're looking to leave Chicago?" I ask before he can jog away from me.

"You barely throw to me; everything goes to Damon. Doesn't sound like my quarterback has my best interests at heart. And a captain who allows his personal shit to interfere with what happens on that field isn't the kind of captain I want." He turns away to head toward the other offensive guys. "Oh, and good luck. I really hope you don't play shitty today, and I say that as a teammate because I want us to win."

He disappears into the crowd of offensive players, and I clench my jaw and start my practice throws. The sad part is he's right. I was so pissed when he was dating Ellery that I always looked for Damon more. It was a shit move, and I'm glad he called me out on it.

"Rice!" a woman's voice screams, and I turn to the stands to see my package being delivered to Ellery.

Bryce gives me a thumbs-up. I watch as Ellery opens up the box and pulls out the necklace that says "I love" with my number. She smiles, and Bryce helps her put it on.

Elle mouths "Thank you, and I love you," and I mouth, "Ditto."

"All this romance shit. What happened to football? Get your head in the game, Rice!" Coach Stone yells as he walks by, having witnessed the scene.

I wink at Ellery and throw the ball again to warm up my arm.

We're down by one with no time-outs, and we have less than a minute on the clock in the fourth quarter. But we have to get the ball down the field. Although I haven't played shitty, things just haven't been going our way in this game. Too many errors by all of us combined. Plus, the Vipers came out like a fucking all-star team today.

I get the play Coach wants and get into the huddle. I tell everyone the play we're making, and Bradley sighs, mumbling, "Could've predicted that one."

I ignore him because we don't have time to fight over this now.

The ball rests on the twenty-five-yard line. Morales hikes the ball to me, and I make a quick throw to Damon, and he runs out of bounds to stop the clock.

The fans go crazy, jumping up and down. We advance fifteen yards, but we need more.

I get the next call and the huddle comes together, Bradley again showing his displeasure that he's not getting the ball.

I throw across the middle to Harris, our tight end, and we hurry up and line up again, the clock continuing to count down. Morales hikes me the ball, and I spike it to stop the clock.

Coach wants me to go to Damon for the next play, but the way the Vipers have been playing tonight, he'll be double-teamed and will have no shot at catching the ball. There's only one hope, and I suck up my ego and do what a good quarterback does.

We huddle together, and I look right at Bradley. "Get open, and this game win is yours."

A smirk comes across his face. I owe him this one, and we both know it.

Morales hikes the ball to me, and I shuffle backward, my eyes on Damon. My offensive line does a killer job of keeping me free for as long as I need, but the clock is ticking down. Right before the timer runs out, I throw a pass downfield to Bradley.

The ball suspends in the air for what feels like forever, but Bradley catches it like every great wide receiver should and brings it into his body, protecting it like a baby. I get tackled to the ground, but I'm really hoping the stadium going crazy means he landed in bounds with the ball.

I quickly scramble to get up from the Vipers' defensive line to see Bradley dancing with Damon in the end zone.

Fuck yeah.

I fist pump in the air and jump up and down. Morales picks me up, cheering.

After I run over and say good game to the guys on the Vipers, I seek out Bradley, but he's already being interviewed. I give him a nod as I walk by, and he nods back to me, a smile on his lips.

Another reporter stops me, and I start talking to them about the last play. I'm in the middle of answering when I catch something behind him that catches his attention. I turn to see Ellery waiting for me.

I reach over and drag her to me, holding her to my side during the interview.

"So, how does it feel that you might be making the best quarterback in the league even better?" The reporter questions Ellery instead of me.

"It was a great catch, too," I interrupt, because Ellery shouldn't have to answer any questions.

"Yes, it was. Well, congratulations on a great game, Cooper. You sure proved those skeptics wrong today."

I shake his hand and turn to Ellery, picking her up in my arms.

"What a game," she says. "You did great."

"I did okay. Not my best, but I didn't choke or play shitty. Not that I thought I would. You've always been my lucky charm." I set her down and tuck her hair behind her ear and bring my lips down to hers.

She kisses me back, and I kick myself for acting like there were problems between us before the game. She never pulls away from me when my hands or lips are on her.

"I'll meet you outside?" she asks.

"I wish you could shower with me," I say, kissing her one last time.

"Later on, I can double-check that you got all the dirt off."

"Perfect." I hold her hand as we slowly walk away from one another, until we have no choice but to separate.

She heads off with Adeline and Bryce, while I head to the locker room.

I'm on cloud nine when we walk out after I'm showered, dressed, and have talked to the press. All I want is to be with Ellery tonight. Clover runs to Damon when we get outside, and he picks her up, kissing her before going to Adeline and hugging her. The three of them leave together.

Bryce tackles Miles, and they head in the direction of the parking lot.

The crowd clears, and I see Bradley and Elle talking. There goes my good mood.

I walk over and wrap my arm around Ellery, kissing her temple before saying hello to him.

"Relax, I was just telling her that I'm happy for you two. That I wasn't ready for the settling down shit yet, so it's good that she secretly loved you." He laughs. "See you guys."

I look at Ellery after he's gone.

She rolls her eyes. "Stop it, you have no reason to be jealous. Take me home."

"Don't have to tell me twice."

I escort her to the Corvette. I've had it out of storage for a few days. I open the passenger-side door to let her in.

"Want to take the long way home?" she asks.

"I can do that."

We haven't ridden in the Corvette since we were a couple and it's too cold to keep the windows down, but there's something that feels right as we drive down Lake Shore Drive snug in the car that I first realized I loved her in.

CHAPTER 23

ELLERY

I rush into the emergency room with my coffee in hand.

"Sorry. Sorry." I jog to the staff locker room and hurriedly get out of my coat, replacing it with my white doctor's coat. The door opens, and I don't take time to see who it is, instead slipping off my boots and putting on my clogs.

Slamming my locker shut, I turn. I thought that maybe Dr. Murphy followed me, but it's my dad.

His hands are stuffed into the pockets of his jacket. "You're late," he says, as if I don't already know.

"The train was behind," I lie, but my dad stares into me as if he knows it was something else.

"I came in early to chat with you because I've heard you've been distracted lately. Imagine my embarrassment when you show up late."

The door opens, and Hayes stands in the doorway with a breakfast sandwich in his hand. He doesn't react right away, his eyes shifting between my dad and me. "I…"

"Leave," my dad says, and Hayes steps back into the hallway, allowing the door to swing shut.

"Jesus, Dad," I say, attaching my badge to my coat.

"Your mother wants you to come over for dinner."

"Okay."

"You and Cooper," he says. "And I wouldn't mind a conversation with him."

Oh god, no.

I narrow my eyes. "Why?"

"This. You being late. Him showing up here from what I hear. The deliveries. This is a hospital, not a social club."

"Who's reporting to you?" I ask, already knowing exactly who it is. "Dr. Murphy? He has it out for me. Always making comments…" I stop myself because I can handle my problems on my own. I don't run to Daddy. But if Dr. Murphy thinks he's going to run to my dad every time he thinks I'm out of line, he'll come to regret it. "It doesn't matter. Cooper has stopped in since I started here, the entire staff gets deliveries, and you're only being like this because I'm your daughter."

"Damn right, I am. Can't you see what you're doing? I saw you after his game on Sunday. Kissing and hugging, being referred to as his girlfriend instead of Dr. Ellery Wallace."

"I can be both," I say, even though his words are playing to my insecurities.

"You worked hard for that title, you should make sure they use it."

I blow out a breath. "Tell Mom to text me about dinner. I have to go start my shift." I walk steadily past him, but he grabs my upper arm and brings me back in front of him.

"I didn't say this conversation was over. Don't embarrass me or yourself. You have a lot of promise here to move up and eventually take over my position when I move up the chain. But if word is reaching me, people won't refrain from telling others." His jaw clenches for a second. "And since when did I not teach you to put this career first? It will reward you and give you a life you can enjoy afterward with

Cooper. You'll get there, but you have to sacrifice. Being known as Cooper Rice's girlfriend isn't going to get you the respect you want or deserve in this industry." He releases me and steps out of the room.

I take a small reprieve to inhale and exhale a few deep breaths. There really is no pleasing him. No matter what I give, it's never enough. I blink back my tears, collect myself, and open the door.

"Thank you for joining us, Dr. Wallace," Dr. Murphy says when I reach the group.

Hayes gives me a sympathetic look that I hate. I don't need anyone's pity. I'm the one who chose to follow my dad to this hospital.

"And Dr. Wallace Senior is joining us this morning. I'm sure you've all already met him. Especially Dr. Wallace." The group laughs at Dr. Murphy's lame joke.

Dr. Mendez isn't here today, so it's Dr. Lim who Dr. Murphy is relieving today, so he runs through the physician handover and gives us the status of each of the patients. There were some shootings last night, and we have two injured teens who have been sent up to surgery. I'm semi-relieved I wasn't here, but I'm thankful they're recovering upstairs instead of being sent downstairs to the morgue.

After that, my dad says he's going to head back to his office for the day.

I'm thankful because I could see him staying here all day just to keep an eye on me like I'm a child.

I go in to see my first patient for the day after being prepped by Dr. Lim. It's a little boy who broke his arm and is waiting for the orthopedic surgeon to take him into surgery.

"Hi, I'm Dr. Wallace, I'm just checking in since we had a shift change."

The mom sits on the bed with the son, and the dad is on the chair.

"Hi," they all say in unison.

"Do we know how much longer?" the dad asks, clearly nervous.

I scan my ID on the computer. "It should be soon. How long have you guys been waiting?"

"Feels like forever," the mom says.

I give them a sympathetic smile because it can be rough here at times.

"Let me call his office," I say. "I can't feed you because of the surgery. Do you want some ice chips?"

"Sure," he says, looking at his mom. "I'm starving."

"Soon. This will all be done soon." She runs her hand through his hair, her eyes looking a little misty.

"I'll step out and see if I can get some answers."

I walk out into the hallway and come to a stop when I see Cooper standing there, holding up my lunch that I forgot in my mad dash out the door. Today is not the day for my dad to see him.

"Thank you," I say, going to the phone and dialing up the orthopedic surgeon's office. "Give me a second."

Then it dawns on me that Cooper can do something while he's here, and it might just make this kid's day. He stands at the counter, his eyes on me, as if he's ready for another round after this morning. I really do have to put my foot down about there being no more sleepovers when I have the early shift.

The surgeon is supposed to be on his way, so I hang up and tell Cooper to wait a second while I peek my head into the room. "Mason, are you a Grizzlies fan?"

His mom lights up, and the color in her cheeks deepens. "Honestly, we did recognize you from last night. You're Cooper Rice's girlfriend, right?" the mom asks, and she's being respectful, but those three words still grate on me.

"I am."

"Well lucky for you, Mason, I forgot my lunch this morning." I step to the door and wave Cooper in. I've done this enough over the years that he has an idea of what he's walking into.

Cooper comes into the room, and all three of their mouths drop open, blinking like they're not really seeing him. I wonder what that feeling is like for Cooper.

"Hey." He shakes the dad's hand. "Cooper Rice," he introduces himself.

"Todd."

The mom says, "I'm Jessica."

"And this is Mason." I gesture to the little boy. "I'll leave you guys to it. I have to check in on another patient. Good news, the surgeon is on his way."

Cooper nods, sitting on the stool beside the bed. "So, tell me, Mason, do you play football?"

Knowing he has this handled, I go to the next room and sanitize my hands again. "Hello, I'm Dr. Wallace."

I continue my rounds, and once I have all my patients in various degrees getting out of the emergency room, the surgeon finally arrives with his resident.

We walk into the room, and Cooper has them all laughing, telling a story about Damon. "Oh, it looks like you're ready." He stands up and fist bumps Mason. "You've got this, and you'll be up playing again in no time, don't worry." After he shakes their hands, he leaves the room.

"Shut up, you're the doctor from Mercy dating Cooper Rice?" the surgeon asks me, his eyebrows raised.

"Yes." Damn, how far has this gossip chain gone?

I leave the room and walk Cooper out to the intake area. "Thanks for that," I say. "And for bringing me lunch."

"Anytime. I love to help out when I can." He leans in and gives me a chaste kiss. "See you tonight?"

I nod. "Yeah, but no sleepover. I was late today."

A sly smile lands on his face, and I shake my head.

"After the season, we're going on a long vacation." He pulls me into him, going in for a kiss.

"I'm at work," I whisper.

Just then I hear a code over at the intake desk about a stabbing victim being en route.

"I'm gonna be late to work out. See you tonight. Love you," he whispers and releases me without kissing me.

"Coop." I stop him. Rushing over, I give him a kiss on the cheek. "Love you."

His smile is so big, I melt for a moment before heading in the back to get prepared for the stabbing victim.

Mason is already being wheeled out of the room to go up and get ready for surgery when I return. "Good luck," I tell him.

His dad rushes over. "You made his day. Please tell Cooper thank you."

"He was happy to do it, but I'll tell him. I'll try to stop by later, but you're in excellent hands."

It's the one part of emergency medicine that I don't always enjoy. The lack of follow-up. Not knowing how the patient does once you treat them and transfer their care elsewhere. Many times, I try to check in, but oftentimes the day gets away from me.

The code comes in again that the stabbing victim is four minutes out.

Dr. Murphy comes over to where the team and I are getting organized. "Me and Wallace are on this one," he says, putting on his disposable gown. I put my own on, and we wait by the ambulance doors.

I can't hold back now that it's just the two of us standing here, the rest of the team a few feet behind. "If you have a problem with me, why don't you just tell me?"

He glances at me and then back to the ambulance area. We can hear the sirens approaching.

"I have no idea what you're talking about, Wallace."

I turn to him. "The tattling about me not being on my game. I fell asleep once, and yes, today I was late, but I'm not the only one. And Cooper has always dropped in no more than other people's family members. And we get sent a lot of food, I'm not sure why you think it's disruptive to the staff." My attempt to keep my anger at bay doesn't work, it's definitely there, and now we're supposed to treat a case together.

"Listen, I know I give you shit, but it's not my style to go tell Daddy. If I have a problem with you, I'll tell you." He turns back to the street again.

I hate this part, waiting to see what kind of case we have. How injured are they, and will we be able to help them? Even with the information from the paramedics, you need to be face-to-face to really see.

"It wasn't you?"

He shakes his head. "Sorry to disappoint you."

"It doesn't disappoint me," I say, though begrudgingly.

"It should." He looks back into the ER. "Because if it wasn't me, it was someone you trust more than me. Maybe even one of your friends."

Just then, the ambulance comes in. No way would anyone do that. I have no problems with anyone. Backing into the spot, the doors of the ambulance open, and we take the stretcher out. The paramedic is in the back, straddling the patient and doing compressions.

Shit.

We wheel the gurney into the hospital, and I was concentrating so much on the information the paramedic was passing on that I didn't notice who the patient was.

Mr. Euing.

CHAPTER 24
COOPER

As I'm finishing my workout, my phone dings in my pocket on the way to my car. It's Ellery. I glance at the time on my phone, she still has hours left in her shift, and that's if she gets off on time.

"Hey, you miss me?"

I hear the stutter of her breath.

"Elle?" I ask, my adrenaline already pumping in my veins. "What's wrong?"

"It's just..." She can barely talk, she's crying so hard. "I just needed to hear your voice."

"What happened?" The last time she called me in hysterics like this, she'd felt responsible for losing a patient who died.

"Mr.... Euing."

The homeless guy that she's grown a relationship with since she was a resident at Mercy. One time she made me drive around looking for him because he hadn't made an excuse to come in for over a month.

"What happened?"

"He's dead. There was..." She heaves for a breath. "Nothing we could do to save him."

"Oh, Elle. I'm sorry. I can head right over there."

"No!" She cries for a few seconds. "I have to finish my shift. Dr. Murphy just told me to take my break."

"I'll be there to pick you up when you're done.

"Thanks." She clears her throat and blows her nose. "Okay, I can do this. I'll see you later today."

"Okay."

She's gotten herself able to go back out there to finish her shift, and I'm not gonna keep harping on whether she's okay. I'll pick her up and take care of her when she's done working. Hopefully, she'll feel a little better by morning.

I bide my time and stop at the grocery store, heading back to my apartment, where I prepare the chocolate chip cookies that I make for her anytime she's feeling down. It started with the very first patient she lost.

I finish just in time to head over to the hospital. There's no way I can be late for her today, so I hope traffic is cooperative.

I decide not to go inside since she said Dr. Murphy's been giving her shit lately. Bringing her lunch is one thing, but picking her up, I can wait outside.

I park my car and wait, not caring that it's a drop-off zone. I'll move if I need to.

She walks out on time, and I get out of the car when I see her coming. When her gaze finds mine, tears fill her eyes, and she walks right into my arms.

I hold her close and kiss the top of her head. "I know. I know how much he meant to you." My hands run up and down her back as sobs rack her body.

Elle appears tough on the outside, like nothing affects her, but it's all a front. She cares for all her patients, but I know Mr. Euing was special to her.

"Come on," I say, opening the passenger door and getting her in the car.

I round the front, ignoring the honks, and climb into the

driver's seat, reaching back and handing her the Tupperware container filled with cookies.

She releases a long breath and smiles over at me. "Thanks."

"Not sure they'll do the trick today, but I wanted to try."

Opening the lid, she holds the container out to me. "No thanks, I had enough of the raw dough."

A small laugh falls out of her because when she's around when I make them, both our fingers are always in the dough. So much so that we only get about half of the cookies baked.

She picks out one with the most chocolate chips and covers up the container, eating it as I drive.

"Is it okay if we go to my place?" I ask, thinking maybe she wants to be in her bed.

"Yeah, but no company," she says.

I reach over and squeeze her knee. "No problem."

I take the long way, hopping on Lake Shore Drive, and turning on the Scorpions "Wind of Change." She closes her eyes and rests her head on the headrest. I don't open the window because it's chilly, but I do drive, and it takes us an extra half hour to get back to my place.

When I pull into the parking garage across from The Den, she shuffles out, and we walk across the street. She's holding up well, but it's that facade that scares me.

She beelines to the couch once we're in my apartment, opening up the container and taking another cookie.

"You want a shower, or do you just want to veg?"

"No, I need a shower." She sighs.

I turn on the water and shut the bathroom door, so it steams up nice for her. She's yet to tell me the specifics of what happened to Mr. Euing, and I learned the first time experiencing this with her to wait until she's ready. Not to rush her through the process because I have no idea what she's going through.

"It's probably ready," I say a few minutes later.

She walks toward the bathroom and goes in, shutting the door behind her. It's then I hear her start to cry again. There's no way I'm letting her face this all on her own, so I strip out of my clothes in my bedroom and open the bathroom door.

"It's just me," I tell her, opening the glass shower door and stepping in behind her.

She's yet to dip her head back to get wet, and when she turns to me, her mascara is streaking down her cheeks more. I run my thumb under her eyes to dry the tears, even though I know more will come.

"Come on, let me," I say, easing her head under the stream of water. When her hair is wet, I take some shampoo in my palms, lathering it up and rubbing it into her blonde hair. My fingers massage her scalp, working the shampoo in. She leans on me, her head tipping forward.

"I should have called the police that day," she says quietly.

"What could they have done?" I ask, tilting her back to rinse the shampoo out of her hair. Once the water runs clear, I take the conditioner, working it through her beautiful locks.

"I don't know, watched the area more, checked the shelters."

"Where did it happen?"

While the conditioner works in her hair, I grab the washcloth and soap, running it over her body to wash her. "The paramedics picked him up right where he always stayed by Nordstrom. You know how he was always fighting for that area." She shakes her head. "I should have done more."

"There's nothing you could've done. He didn't want your help." Again, I nudge her head back to rinse the conditioner out and the rest of her body off.

I turn off the water and wrap my arms around her, but she begins to shiver. I grab a towel, holding it out for her. She walks into my waiting arms, and I wrap the warmth around her. She turns and steps into me, and I hold her. Hell, I'll hold her for a lifetime if she'll let me.

We go into the bedroom, and I dress her in one of my sweatshirts that hangs down to her knees and a pair of my pajama pants she has to roll five times at the waist. Turning back my sheets and comforter, she slips into bed, and I join her after dressing in my sweats and turning on the television. Although she might not laugh, she always asks for a comedy with Vince Vaughn in it during times like this because she doesn't want to wallow.

I turn on *The Break-Up,* and she cuddles into my chest. I wrap my arms around her, wishing I could take the pain away for her.

A half hour later, I feel her body go limp, and I wiggle over to see that she's asleep. Not wanting to leave her, I stay there until my door buzzer rings. I slide out of bed, turning down the volume so it doesn't wake her up.

Damon stands on the other side of the door.

"What's wrong?" He doesn't look like he has good news.

"Hey man, can I come in?"

I glance inside my apartment. Damon is notorious for being loud. "Mind if we talk out here. Elle is sleeping, and today was a hard day. She lost a patient."

He frowns. "Oh shit, I'm sorry. Yeah, of course. I mean, I'd tell you later, but time is of the essence with this."

"Okay. Let me just grab my coat or something." I rush inside, grabbing my coat and coming right back. "What's up?"

"Remember how I announced that we were looking at houses?" He shuffles his feet. "Well, we got the one we wanted, and we had to do a fast closing to get it. I'll totally pay you for the rest of my lease, but for Clover's sake, we're moving sooner rather than later."

Man, it feels like the end of an era. Damon's lived here almost as long as I have.

"It won't be the same without you."

He nods a few times, appearing somber about the whole

change himself. "Crazy, I thought I might live here forever since I never planned any of this." He looks in the direction of his apartment. "But we've discussed wanting to have another kid. We're not sure Clover is the type of kid who can wait to have to share our attention with a sibling. I love her so much, but she's defiant."

"You've spoiled her," I say, not that I can't see myself doing the same thing. My eyes stray to the inside of the apartment to where my future lies tucked in bed.

"Yeah, lesson learned." He chuckles because we both know he probably won't change.

"And no worries about the rent, you aren't paying if you aren't living here. I'm sure I can find someone. I'm happy for you and your family."

He shoves his hands in his pockets. "It'll be weird not living with you and another teammate. I mean, we have our own places, but fuck, it's time to grow up I guess, huh?"

I laugh. "You act like we're not going to see one another. We play for the same team, and our wi… well, your wife and my girlfriend, along with Miles's wife, are all friends. They'll be making plans for all of us."

He chuckles. "Yeah, they will."

"You won't miss me that much." I squeeze his shoulder.

"I will miss your cheap rent. If I told you how much we're paying for this mortgage." He shakes his head.

"You really want me to feel sorry for you? You have plenty of money."

He runs his hand over his head and pulls at his neck. "Yeah, we're fortunate, but still, I don't know how people do it who don't make what we do." He shakes his head. "Since when did we start grumbling about mortgage payments and how expensive stuff is? What the hell is happening to me?"

"You started it."

"We're getting old. You better catch up."

I don't say anything because Elle doesn't work like that,

and although I'd have us married tomorrow, I'm trying like hell to take this slow for her.

"Go and be with her. I'll let you know a specific date, but we'll be out soon."

"Great. Thanks."

We shake hands, and he heads back to his place. This day just got shittier, although I understand why Damon and Adeline need to find a place in the city big enough for Clover and however many other kids they end up having. Something tells me it might be a lot.

I shut the door of my apartment and find Ellery still asleep on my bed, looking peaceful. Stopping in the doorway, I take my time to soak in her beauty. I don't deserve her, but damn if I'm ever going to give her up. I just have to convince myself that it's okay not to rush her to accept my ring and my last name. I thought that if we ever got together, things would be perfect. I never thought I'd struggle as much as I have these weeks that we've been together. But it's only because I love her so much.

CHAPTER 25

ELLERY

"You've had dinner with my parents plenty of times, why would you be nervous?" I sit on the counter of his bathroom and grab each end of his tie.

"It's different now. I'm your boyfriend, not just your friend." He watches me in the reflection of the mirror. Although we both know the student has surpassed the teacher in regard to knotting a tie.

I'd asked him to teach me years ago, and we practiced almost the entire day, so now every time I'm around, I do his ties. This is the first time since we've been a couple, and I like the way his hands rest on my legs, his thumbs running back and forth along my skin. The fact I'm sitting here in a pair of silk underwear and a bralette proves how far we've come.

My parents demanded we go to the club for dinner—probably to show off Cooper to their friends—but I didn't fight them on it because I can tell my dad sees Cooper as a problem when it comes to my future. Cooper isn't going to be like my mom and keep a good house and raise our kids and wait until I come home. Nor would I want that. I want to be an active part of my kids' lives, unlike my dad, who was only really involved when it came to big decisions, and even then, he dictated more than discussed.

"My mom loves you, and she's thrilled we're together."

"And your father?" He eyes me.

"He's happy—ish." I laugh.

"Exactly. And you know I'm at a disadvantage there with all of his friends." I finish, and of course he takes it in his hands and messes with it as if I didn't straighten it enough.

I move to slide off the counter, not ready yet, but his large hand stops me.

"Not so fast," Cooper says. "Thank you."

He leans forward, and I press both hands on either side of his face, kissing him. Nothing deep or uncontrollable, just a little peck.

"Why are you prancing around this apartment in hardly anything?" His gaze falls down my body, and I instinctively push out my breasts.

He raises his hand and molds over my lace-covered breast, his thumb brushing over my nipple. I moan, and he brings his other hand up, doing the same thing with my other breast.

"You're so damn sexy," he whispers, although we're alone in my apartment.

I place both my palms on the countertop and push myself back up as he bends down, and our lips meet. He steps in closer, and my legs wrap around his waist, our kiss deepening. Will there ever be a time I don't want this man? Common sense says yes, but how was I only friends with him for ten years?

He strips his lips off me. "Yeah, we're gonna be late."

I giggle as he picks me up by my ass and carries me out of the bathroom into my bedroom. Dropping me on the mattress, he fiddles with his belt, but I place my hands on his.

"Allow me. We don't want you all wrinkly." I give him my best seductress look through my eyelashes.

Coming to the edge of the bed, I unbuckle his belt,

unbutton his pants, and as I'm lowering the zipper, his hand cradles my face, his thumb running over my lips. Damn him and his ability to make me even hotter. At this point, I'm changing my thong before I go out.

"Fuck, babe," he says like he's about to come.

The flaps of his slacks open, and I slide my hand in, taking out his throbbing dick. I hold it in place with my hand, guiding it to my mouth. I lick up his shaft and cover the tip with my mouth, causing him to jolt.

I take him in inch by inch, swallowing just as the tip hits the back of my throat. His hand tightens on my face, and I'm glad he's staying away from my hair. I don't have time to redo it again.

"That's it, Elle." His tone is soft and seductive, turning me on even more, and I slowly release him, only to do the exact same thing again. I keep him as far back in my throat as I can. One thing I've discovered about Cooper is how much he loves it when I blow him. And I know that when we really get going, he's going to fuck my face. It's hot as hell making a guy who has control over everything in his life crazy. On the field, his finances, his private life—but as soon as my mouth is on him, he loses it all, and I revel at being the one to cause it.

Just as I thought, I remove my hand from his shaft, and he grabs both sides of my face pulling me off and on his dick, the sloppy sound echoing through the room.

"Damn," he says. "Your mouth... never enough... god. Tell me if I'm too rough."

I shake my head, and his eyes focus on mine as he uses me to get himself off. "I'm coming," he says a second later.

I nod, and he pumps into me three more times before he stills and pumps his release into my mouth. Once I finish swallowing, I slowly move my mouth off his dick.

"You'd tell me if I hurt you?" There's so much concern in his eyes.

I chuckle and nod. "Yes."

He picks me up and tosses me further onto the bed. "Now it's my turn. Spread your legs."

"We can't be late." I really just wanted him to be relaxed when he had to meet with my dad. You never know what's going to come out of his mouth.

"If you think I'm gonna let you blow me, and I'm not gonna bury my head between your legs, you're crazy." His palms slide up my legs, parting them until he teases me over the crotch of my thong, sliding it over and dipping his head between my legs.

The man is good at everything, including going down on women. Part of me hates the women who have come before me, but then again, I'm thankful that I'm with him now. Those others don't matter. They were fill-ins because he's always wanted me like I want him.

It only takes five minutes before I'm screaming. God knows what my neighbors must think these days.

He puts my panties back in place and smirks as he lifts himself from between my thighs. "Good?"

"Cocky ass," I say, getting up and putting my arms around his neck. "You know you're good at that."

"I'm just happy you enjoyed it." He gives me a quick kiss and heads into the bathroom.

I changed my underwear and put on my emerald green dress. Knowing my parents' country club, there will be dancing, and I'm excited to slow dance with Cooper.

We head down from my apartment to the car he ordered for us. We have to head north to the suburbs where my parents live, and neither one of us wanted to drive.

We climb in, and I really hope he's more relaxed because my stomach is a bundle of nerves, worried about what exactly my dad might say to him tonight.

My mom spots us as soon as we enter the club. She excuses herself from the couple she's talking to and wraps us both in her arms. Both of us have to bend down to her height, and she practically puts us in headlocks. "Oh, you two look gorgeous together."

She kisses each of our cheeks and finally releases us, both of us having to find our footing after. For being small, she's strong.

She looks us over again, her eyes filling with happiness. "I just can't believe it."

"Stop gushing over them, Dana." My dad walks over to me first, putting his hand on my back and kissing my cheek. "Green has always been your color." He extends his hand to Cooper. "Glad you could both make it."

"Thank you for having us, Dr. Wallace," Cooper says, polite as always.

"No more of that. Call me Ryan."

I glance at my dad, surprised that he's allowing Cooper to call him Ryan now that we're dating when, for the past ten years, it's always been Dr. Wallace.

"I heard about that homeless fellow you like. I'm sorry," my dad says to me.

Cooper comes to my side and wraps his arm around my waist. I see my dad clocking it. He has no idea how much Cooper helped me that day. Losing a patient is horrible, let alone one that you've made friends with. I have no idea how family care or specialists deal with the losses.

"Sweetie, I'm sorry." My mom's lips turn into a frown. "That's a shame."

"Yeah. I keep thinking I should've done more."

My dad shakes his head. "You can't think like that. We're there for medical treatment, not to get people extra help outside of those doors. People make their choices, Ellery."

"I know." I've heard this speech enough through the years. I can see why my dad picked emergency medicine. You get the patient good enough to either be transported to another office or to send them home. I'm starting to think that I want to be more involved in their care.

"Let's sit and eat." My mom heads over to a table of four.

At least none of the other members are joining us. I hate it when they do. It's just not my scene.

Cooper pulls out my chair for me as my dad does my mom's.

"Thanks," I say, and he smiles, sitting in his own chair.

"You're welcome."

We all look over the menu, the waiter comes over, and Cooper and I agree to have the same wine my parents are having. My dad orders another bottle.

"Let's toast to the two of you." My mom raises her wine class. "It's about time you two saw through that friendship facade. Welcome to the family, Cooper." She smiles genuinely at him, and we all clink glasses.

"Yes, what did change to take you two from just being friends to more?" my dad asks.

Cooper and I share a look.

"It was that Bradley, wasn't it?" my mom asks. "I told Ryan as soon as I heard that it was going to spur Cooper into action if he really wanted our daughter." She playfully pats Cooper's forearm.

"That's part of it, but I think we just got out of each other's way." Cooper shrugs. "But I was seething with jealousy seeing the two of them together, especially when she showed up at the game with his jersey on."

My mom laughs and sips her wine. "I love it. I never could make this one jealous." She glances at my dad. "His first love is medicine. So, it's me being jealous until he retires. Even then, he'll probably find some way to keep his toe in it." She's laughing, but I saw the times when Dad didn't show up at my concerts or soccer games. When she'd have to make excuses and pretend it didn't bother her. Or the nights he was supposed to be home, and she'd make a big dinner only for the two of us to eat at the breakfast bar. She always put on a good face, and I never knew differently until I was in high school.

"Oh stop it, Dana, you know I love you." My dad sips his wine.

She smiles up at him. "I know you love me, but I also know what you love more."

I cross my fingers that this doesn't turn into a conversation about dedication and how he cannot just leave in the middle of a case. That it's not a nine-to-five job. Plus, I'm not sure how much more I want Cooper to overhear, although he's already aware of how my schedule changes.

"I have another announcement," my dad says.

I look at my mom, and she shrugs, looking questioningly at my dad. Cooper's hand finds my thigh, and he squeezes.

"What is it?" I ask.

"I just accepted a position at Sherman Hope in New York as Chief Medical Officer for them."

He's so excited that we all numbly push our glasses toward the middle of the table in cheers.

"But dad…"

He raises his hand at me. "Don't worry, guess what position I'm filling first?"

I've never seen him so happy before.

"What?"

"Head of Emergency Medicine, and something tells me it's yours."

Cooper's wine glass slips from his hands, but he grabs it right before it falls, only a splash of wine landing on the tablecloth.

I swallow at the sudden dryness in my throat. "What are you talking about?"

"Yes, Ryan, because you never discussed this with me. I have friends here, and the last place I want to live is in New

York." My mom downs the rest of her wine and reaches for the bottle, but Cooper grabs it first and refills her drink for her.

My dad totally ignores my mom's comment. "I've already told them how I want you with me. Yes, the hospital is a little smaller than Mercy, but you're going to love it there. The patient care is wonderful."

"I'm not leaving Chicago," I say, but at the back of my mind, I'm thinking about how being the head of emergency medicine at my age would be insane. Am I even ready for something like that?

"Why not? We just need to get Cooper traded to New York, or better yet, you can live separately for the season. You can still see one another." My dad smiles across the table at me.

"It's a great opportunity," Cooper says.

I'm not sure if he means it or not, but his smile is genuine.

How do I leave him when we're just getting started? A long-distance relationship doesn't seem like the best decision for us, but then again, maybe it would be a natural way to slow down our trajectory.

CHAPTER 26
COOPER

I really hope my face shows the excitement I have for her and not how sad I am thinking of her living so far away from me. I won't be able to stop in at the hospital or meet her after work. We're just so early in our romantic relationship—can it survive the long distance?

Ellery can't know my doubts because this is an opportunity she shouldn't pass up.

We're on our way home now, and she didn't really give her father an answer. I think maybe Ryan Wallace should've talked to his wife first before he decided to spring the news on everyone.

"So?" I ask Ellery since she's been staring out the window the entire ride home.

"I'm not sure what to do. I mean, Dr. Murphy gives me shit all the time about me working under my dad, would the staff in New York even like me knowing I got the job from my daddy?"

I reach over and grab her hand, my thumb gliding over her pointer finger. "It's not like you're not deserving. And no matter what, people will claim favoritism if you work with your dad regardless of what your role is."

"I just didn't see this coming. I get that my dad wants to move up, and I'm guessing Mercy dragged their feet too long, and now he's gone in search of something else because of his ridiculous timeline."

"Timeline?"

"My dad has age markers of where he wants to be at certain ages. He's about to be fifty-five, and he wants to be the chief of medicine for a hospital. So…"

It's so different from how I think. I go season by season. How hurt and banged up am I when the season ends? Do I think I can handle another one? Can I still perform my best? And when it's over, I'm going to miss it like crazy, but I hope to have a family waiting for me, and then I'll get to be part of my kids' lives as they grow up.

"He really is a go-getter," I say because I'm not sure what else to say.

I don't want to voice the thought that I think her dad could be making this move to get her away from me. He sees me as some shiny object that pulls her focus away from her career.

"Am I stupid for considering it?" She has a worried expression on her face.

"No, it's an amazing opportunity." I want to throw up.

"And what about us?" she asks.

"I only play for half the year, and I can live in New York the other half of the time. We'll have to try to make it work when I'm in season." I hold myself back from speaking my biggest worry—what if we forget what it is about the other person that we can't live without?

"True. We couldn't ask for you to have a more flexible job to make it work."

Jesus, why am I convincing her?

Because maybe she'll miss me when she's gone and want all those things I want, like marriage and kids, sooner?

Because I'll be able to focus on my own game and achieve

that third championship win and hopefully MVP? If I did both those things, I'd seriously consider retiring and moving to New York with her. But do I want that? I'm not sure.

"Can I even handle the responsibility?" She groans, turning to me and snuggling up to my side.

"You can do anything. You're an intelligent, amazing woman." Which is true. I've never met anyone like Elle who can adapt to different situations so well. She'll learn the ropes and do well, and people will love her. Sure, she'll run into some Dr. Murphy's along the way, but she has to get over that.

"You're saying that because you love me."

"The fact that I love you goes without saying."

She looks up at me. "I'm really thinking about it." She cringes as if she's scared, which I'm sure she is.

"Good." I glance out the window so she can't see through me. But as always, I'm too transparent to her.

"Coop?" She straddles my lap and uses her hands to direct my face forward. "Talk to me."

I place my hands on her hips just as we hit a pothole, saving her head from hitting the top of the car. "It's just the usual insecurities that I'm not going to give any attention to. If you want to go, you go. We'll figure out the rest."

"Are you sure?" Her gaze roams my face.

This is the time if I'm going to be honest, but if I go with honesty, I'll mess this up between us. She deserves to have it all, no matter how it affects me. I refuse to hold her back. "Definitely. Take the job."

She squeals and leans down to kiss me. "I'm going to sleep on it tonight, but I think I'm going to. Think of how much fun we'll have going around New York, finding great restaurants, Broadway, and all the excitement. We'll have so much fun when you visit." She wraps her arms around my neck. "Thank you so much. I love you."

Her hips move over my crotch, and for the first time in

weeks, my dick has no reaction to it. I think, like me, it's scared to death of what the future holds.

"Hey, I'm Cooper." I open the building's door and put my hand out to the guy I'm showing Damon's apartment to.

"Rowan Landry, thanks for showing me the place. I'm glad Jagger told me about this place when I got traded. You won't mind a hockey guy living in The Den?"

I laugh.

My agent, Jagger, came into town two days ago and told me how he had a client who was traded to the Chicago Falcons hockey team and needed an apartment. I told him about Damon moving out, and hopefully this meet and greet will be enough for me to find someone to rent it.

"We might have to change the name to the Bird's Nest or something. Though there will be fewer women loitering around these days since Miles and I are taken."

He laughs. "Are you suggesting football has more game than hockey?"

I shrug. "Can't blame them. We have all our teeth and usually don't leave the field bloody."

"The girls like the blood. The teeth, probably not so much, but girls get hot for the fights. You guys go after one another, and the refs stop it immediately. And I won't even say anything about quarterbacks sliding to the ground to make sure they won't be tackled."

I knock on the apartment door. Damon and Adeline are out.

"Actually." He pulls out his phone. "Can you wait one second? I have a teammate who's in the area and wants to see the place with me. He just got here."

"Sure."

He jogs down to the gates and I stand by the door. Ellery

is in New York, interviewing for the job today. Her dad's already started at Sherman Hope. She's still at Mercy, and Dr. Murphy took Dr. Wallace's position. If all goes well today, Ellery will put in her notice and be gone in two weeks. I'm not prepared for her to leave me.

I hear two bodies walk up the stairs, already laughing and having a good time together.

Holy shit, when he said teammate, I didn't think he was talking about Tweetie Sorenson.

"Hey, Tweetie," he introduces himself when they make it to the apartment door.

I wonder what his real name is if the man is introducing himself to me using his nickname.

"Cooper," I say.

"Yeah, I know." He smiles. "Awesome place you have here. Miles Cavanagh up on the top, and Siska's moving out with his girl, huh?"

"You a football fan?" I chuckle.

"Jagger told me I should be here for the tour in case another one of you moves, and I want in."

"Let me show you the apartment. All three are the same, but there's no elevator, so the top floor is a hike." I insert the key into the lock and open the door.

Damon and Adeline have already started packing, so there are boxes sitting around, but it's neat and clean for me to show.

"So, this is Siska's life now, huh?" Tweetie looks at the toy corner, shaking his head. "We used to be in the same circle a couple of years ago. He was the biggest partier and reminded me a lot of—"

"Ford Jacobs?" Rowan asks.

"Yeah. Both of those fuckers have wealthy families."

"And both became daddies from one-night stands," I add.

Tweetie snaps and points at me. "That's right."

They walk around a bit and take a look at everything.

"The place is great. Two bedrooms, not a huge building, close to everything. I'll take it," Rowan says.

"That was easy," I joke.

"Well, personally, if you guys can live here and at least have *some* privacy, that's all I'm looking for."

Tweetie puts his arm around Rowan's shoulder. "This guy is like you for the Falcons. He's the heartthrob all the women want."

Rowan almost appears embarrassed but doesn't deny it.

"They're out at the end of the week, so whenever you want to move in, it's yours. I'll hire a cleaning crew in between."

"Great. I'll give my current place two weeks' notice, although I think they want me out sooner than later." I must look confused because he continues on. "The women in the building stop by my apartment all the time. Sometimes they loiter around my door when I'm not home. And my neighbor across the way is done with it. She's taken it to management, and somehow they see me as the problem."

"That's a rough one. You won't experience that here. I'll take you down and introduce you to Ruby at Peeper's Alley. She throws the women out if they become a bother."

"Perfect."

I take them downstairs to Peeper's Alley. All the men turn around in their stools and look at Rowan and Tweetie before turning back around to watch the old TV above the bar.

Ruby comes by. "Who are your friends, Cooper?" I'm not sure how much this group watches hockey.

"They play for the Falcons. Rowan Landry and Tweetie Sorenson."

"Tweetie, did your mom not like you or something?" Ruby asks.

They all chuckle. "It's my nickname on the ice."

"Are you a gossiper?"

"No. I chirp at my opponents all the time." He grins.

"I like that then." Her eyes go to Rowan. "You've got one?"

"Um..."

"Magic," Tweetie tells her. We all look confused, and Rowan lowers his gaze to the ground. "He's got moves on the ice like Magic Mike."

"Stripper moves?" Ruby asks, and I'm surprised she even knows the movie *Magic Mike*.

"Not really, he's just really smooth," Tweetie says, laughing so hard it's contagious.

"Well welcome, Rowan. You seem quiet, and I like quiet." She looks pointedly at Tweetie. "You, on the other hand, not so much."

"Why?" He follows her closer to the bar, and I tell Rowan to follow me so I can show him our private room in case fans find him. What I'm not prepared for is to find Ellery in the room with Bryce, her suitcase by the door.

She got back and came to see Bryce instead of me? This isn't a good start.

CHAPTER 27

ELLERY

The door to the backroom at Peeper's Alley opens, and my stomach drops, because without looking behind me, I know Cooper is there. I can *feel* him.

"Elle?" he says.

Bryce's hand squeezes mine, and she lets me go. "Who are your guests, Cooper?"

I turn around to face him. Bryce is my savior for giving me time to process everything I just told her.

"This is Rowan Landry and Tweetie Sorenson," he answers.

"I was kidding. I know who Rowan *and* Tweetie are. I'm the sports reporter, remember?" Bryce acts offended, and I'm not sure if she's doing it because she really is or if she's still helping me by stalling.

"You reported on the Tundra, not the Falcons." Cooper appears pissed since he's talking to Bryce, but his eyes haven't left mine yet.

"I'm aware, but now I report on the Grizzlies, and I feel like maybe an unflattering article about their quarterback is due." She juts out her hip and stares him down.

"Can we talk at your place?" I ask him.

He sighs. "Rowan, this is Miles Cavanaugh's wife, Bryce. She's a reporter, so be careful. I'll be in touch about move-in dates." All three men shake hands, and Cooper wheels my suitcase out the other door into the back hall, where we can get to his apartment without having to go to the street.

He doesn't say anything, asks me no questions on the way to his apartment, and once we're behind the closed door, he wheels my suitcase to the side and goes into the kitchen. "Want something to drink?"

"Water would be great."

He meets me by the couch and hands me the water.

"You're back early," he says.

If he's offended that I didn't call him to pick me up from the airport, he doesn't mention it, but I had to talk to someone who wasn't him. As much as he was the first person I wanted to call after the news, I needed to run it by someone else first.

"Yeah, it didn't take as long as I thought, and I was able to fly standby on an earlier flight."

"And how did it go?"

"It went really well." I force a smile.

He puts on a smile himself, but I'm not stupid, it isn't his genuine one. "That's great. They give you everything you want?"

"They took me on a tour of the hospital, and although their emergency room is a tad smaller than Mercy's and can't handle the same triage we can there, it's busy. The other doctors were nice and knew who I was, that I was the daughter of the new chief. I mean, they could have been being fake, but no one said anything. The salary is more than I make now, a lot more. And the hours are a little better. I'd be responsible for a lot of things, not just patients."

"So…" He seems to hold his breath while he waits for me to answer.

"I accepted the job." Now I hold mine.

"Oh."

"My dad was pressing me for a decision, and he took me to the airport and was telling me how great it is to take this step so young. How I'll beat his milestones by ten years if I take this job. And…"

I don't want to tell him why I wanted to talk to Bryce. I don't want him to think my dad isn't behind us, although I got the gist today that maybe he's not. I want us to keep this relationship going, I know we're strong enough.

"Why did you call Bryce before me?" Hurt is all over his face—in the downturned angle of his lips, in the crease between his brows, and in the glisten of his eyes.

I stand, unable to sit any longer. "I just needed another opinion, one that wasn't yours, and I say that out of my love for you. This is coming at a horrible time for us, and I don't expect you to be happy about it."

"But I am." He stays seated on the chair. "I'm on your side here, Elle."

"My dad thinks we should take a break." I spit out what he told me right before I got out of the car at the airport.

"What?" He stands but doesn't come over to me. Doesn't reassure me, instead, he goes to the cabinet and grabs some whiskey, pouring himself a shot before downing it. I've never known Cooper to drink like that. "And what did you say? 'Okay, Daddy?'"

His words slice through me like an arrow.

He pours another shot and slams it back.

"Cooper…"

"What? I just think that you listen to him a lot more than you do yourself. Or maybe it's me who isn't listening to what you've been saying."

I shake my head, wondering how this has all gotten away from us. Days ago, he was telling me that he was on board, that we'd survive this.

He crosses his arms over his chest. "Can I ask you a question?"

"What?"

"On your dad's little 'timeline,' did he leave any room for you to get married?" He puts timeline in air quotes.

"It's not my timeline, it's his."

"But he's telling you to leave me so that you can be ten years ahead of him. Is that what you want?"

I open my mouth and shut it. "I don't know."

He nods, pouring another shot and downing it. "Funny, you don't know that, but you do know that you aren't interested in marrying me or having children any time soon. Nor do you want to live together. What you do want is to dictate how many times I see you in a week. You're pretty fucking clear on where *we* stand, but not your career. The career you're traveling miles away from everything and everyone you know for."

"You told me if I took this job, it wouldn't affect us. That we'll be fine." Hurt wars with anger in my chest.

"Yes, but I also think maybe you're taking this job, using it as an out. Ever since we got together, something is keeping you one foot out, and I don't know what it is. I love you, and I've loved you for a decade, but maybe your feelings for me aren't the same, aren't as strong." He downs another shot and pushes it all away, going back to his chair and staring down at the floor.

"I love you. I am in this." My voice is growing louder.

"With stipulations of how much I'm allowed to love you."

I'm growing madder the more he talks as if I'm not in this. "I don't know what you're talking about. I've been in this one hundred percent from the start. Yes, did I want to date you? I did because I wanted to know what it was like. And I'm not ready for marriage and kids. We've literally been dating for like two months."

"And we've known each other for over ten years!" he shouts.

I sit down on the couch. "I'm not sure what you want from me."

"Nothing." He raises his head, and he looks at me. "That's the thing, I never wanted one thing from you. Actually, no, strike that. All I ever wanted was your love. That's it."

"You have it, Cooper. I love you."

"So much so that you can't wait to get away from me."

"You told me to take it!" I shout in frustration.

"The minute your dad brought it up, I saw it in your eyes. The excitement. The wanting to please him. Never once did you think how it might interfere with us. It's not that I think I should be the basis for your decision, but it would be nice to think that maybe I factored in even a little."

He's implying something without actually saying it, and if we're going to move forward, I want to hear it.

"Spit it out, Coop."

He throws his hands up in front of him. "I don't think you feel the same for me as I do for you. I think you got caught up in it all, and after we got together, you got scared. That's why you suddenly wanted to put some rules down. But I'm a big boy, Elle. I can handle someone not loving me the way I love them. Ten years ago, when you asked to just be my friend because you always wanted me in your life, I wish you would've just told me the truth—that you didn't feel the same way I did."

"What are you talking about?" I ask, my voice low because I don't understand what he's doing. He's taking a wrecking ball and aiming it right at our relationship, but I don't understand why.

"I'm talking about the sacrifices I would make for you. Anything, Elle, I'd do anything as long as you were in my life. Quit football. Done."

"I'd never ask that of you."

"Just like I'm not asking you to quit, I'm asking you to include me in your life and your life decisions. You're my entire future. I see no one else, but to you, I feel like a fresh relationship. I want you to have everything you want, Elle, but your actions don't say that you're one hundred percent on board with us. Not to mention, all you do is complain about all the shit you have to take at work because of your dad, and now you're following him when this could be your time to get out from under him."

I blow out a breath and stare at him. "So what then? Where do we go from here?"

He sits up in the chair, resting his forearms on his legs, and stares at the floor. "I think we take a break."

My heart stills in my chest. "Seriously?"

He lifts his head, and he stares at me for a moment. "You need time to think about what you want, especially from this relationship. You can't control my feelings. I want marriage and kids with you. I want you to have it all, the career and the family and anything else you want in this life. But I'm not sure it's what you want, and even if you do, whether I'm the one you want it with."

He stands. "Go to New York. We waited ten years. What's a little more time?"

"Cooper," I say, walking toward him, but he puts his hand up in the air.

"I can't do it, Elle. I can't come second. Not when I'd put you first every damn second of my life. I want to share my life with someone, not feel like I'm dragging them along for the ride." He turns to leave.

"I never meant…"

He opens up his apartment door and shuts it quietly. He might as well have slammed it shut because it feels like the finality of our relationship.

CHAPTER 28

COOPER

Maybe I'm an idiot. I've never been so mad and disappointed in my life, and never would I have thought it'd be directed at Elle.

Jogging down the stairs, I zip up my jacket and push through the iron gates. Instead of heading to Peeper's Alley, I walk down the block to one of the trendier bars.

I saddle up to the bar and ask the bartender for a shot of whiskey and a beer.

He nods and does me a solid by not saying he recognizes me.

My phone vibrates in my pocket, but I ignore it, continuing to drink and mindlessly watch the television that's replaying some show about the stupid shit that people do.

A woman saddles up next to me. "Cooper Rice?"

I glance over at her. She's a cute brunette dressed in jeans and a short crop top that shows off her stomach. Her hair is braided to the side. I remember when Elle used to do that with her hair. Back when she wasn't mine, but I wanted her to be.

"Yeah." I sip my beer. No reason to deny it.

"You don't mind if I sit here, do you?" She circles on the stool.

"It's not my bar." I lift the shot glass, and the bartender brings the bottle down. I slide my credit card over to start a tab.

"I'm Flora," she says, jutting her hand out.

I shake it and return my hand to my beer.

"You want to talk about it?"

"No." I down the shot.

"Want to talk about anything?"

"No." I keep my gaze on the TV.

"You certainly aren't showing me a side that would make me want to cheer for the Grizzlies."

I swivel in my stool to face her. "Listen, I'm having a real bad fucking day. The last thing I need is some girl hitting on me. I plan on drinking until I'm numb, so I'd go find some other guy to hit on tonight."

She stares at me for a beat. "You know the best way to get over someone is to get under someone else. Why don't we go back to my place, and I promise you I can make you forget all about her."

I used to be surprised by these advances, but not so much anymore.

"That's not my style."

She shakes her head. "Of course, the one player I meet isn't into fucking around."

My phone vibrates again, and I pull it out just to get away from this woman.

"I even gave you a fake name." She picks up her drink and finishes it.

"What?" I answer my phone when I see that it's Miles, hoping this woman will get out of here.

"Where the hell are you? Why is Ellery in tears?"

"Don't worry about it."

"I thought you were cool with her taking the job?"

"I don't want to talk about it. See you at practice tomorrow." I hang up on him and nod at the bartender.

"What a waste," Flora, or whatever her name is, says, slamming her glass on the bar top and walking away.

Thank God.

I move away from the bar and into a booth, giving myself more privacy.

I don't know how long I'm there when two bodies slide in on either side of me. But I know it's long enough for all the alcohol I've ingested to hit me.

"Guys!" I raise my beer. "Have a drink."

As luck would have it, my waitress, Carmen, comes to take their drink order. "What will you guys have?"

"Just a water," Miles says.

"Nothing," Damon answers and turns his gaze on me. "What the fuck?"

"What?" I glare at him.

"What is wrong with you? You're getting drunk during the week, and we have practice tomorrow. The girl you've been drooling over for years is crying uncontrollably back at The Den. I'm watching you ruin your entire life."

"She doesn't love me, man," I say, finishing off my beer.

"Ellery said that?" Miles's eyebrows raise.

"She didn't have to. It's obvious in her actions. She doesn't want marriage or kids, or at least not with me."

Carmen comes over, and I ask her for another beer, but Miles shakes his head. "If you want a big tip, you'll refill my drink," I tell her.

Damon reaches into his pocket and pulls out a couple hundred-dollar bills. "This is to not serve him anymore."

Carmen's eyebrows shoot up, and she smiles. "Done."

"Traitor. All you women are traitors!" I shout after her.

"Whoa now, let's not get kicked out of the bar," Damon says.

"I love her," I say, the crack in my voice belying how

scared I am that I might lose it. "But she doesn't love me the same way."

"How do you know?" Miles asks.

"Because she's first in my world, but I'm not in hers. She wants space and not to rush into things, but we've been best friends for ten fucking years. I know her cycle, her favorite brand of makeup, how much she dislikes poppy seed bagels but loves poppy seed muffins. I would ace a trivia quiz about Ellery Wallace."

Neither of them says anything.

"And now she's gonna move? To New York? Like her dad didn't set that up to get her away from me."

"I doubt—" Miles starts to say when I shoot him a death glare.

"He told her today on the way to the airport that she should take a break from me. That there's always time for relationships, but if she wants to get where she wants to be in her career, she can't have me tagging along."

"Fucking hell." Damon looks at Miles. "Adeline's mom was rough at first, but she never told Adeline to kick me to the curb. I'd be pissed too."

"But what did Ellery say about it? Did she agree?" Miles asks.

"She flew in early, and instead of coming to talk to me about it, she chose to go to Bryce. Which tells me she was thinking about what her dad said, that she didn't know what to do."

I lift my empty mug and try to get the last drop of beer out of it.

"Now you just look pathetic." Damon takes the glass from my hands.

"You sure are assuming a lot," Miles says.

I shake my head. "I know Elle. I know how her brain works."

"Okay," he says, accepting that I know her best. Better

than even Bryce. She might not have been thinking about it consciously, but there's a reason she sought out Bryce.

My head suddenly feels heavy, and then my forehead hits the wood table.

"Let's go," one of them says.

"He paid up?" Damon must ask the waitress.

"He put it all on a tab," Carmen says.

"Leave yourself a one hundred percent tip."

My head lifts to argue, but it falls back down. I need a bed.

We all slide out of the booth on one side, each of them taking the weight of half of my body and escorting me out of the bar.

"AGAIN!" Coach Stone screams.

We run the play again. I'm like an elderly man with a walker with my speed out of the pocket, and when I throw the ball, it gets caught by an orange shirt.

Coach Stone throws his clipboard. "God damn it, Rice! What the hell is wrong with you?"

"I've got a headache," I say.

"Then take some pain medicine. I'm not your fucking mommy. Get off the field. Give me Beacon. Rice, go sit your ass on the bench."

I go to the bench, throw my helmet on the ground, and sit down, cursing to myself.

I've never gotten drunk the night before a practice. Sure, maybe a few drinks, but I've never woke up with cottonmouth and my body aching. I'm sure the heartbreak isn't helping me either. I wish Ellery would have been at my place when I got home last night.

Suddenly, overwhelming nausea hits my stomach, and I run to the trashcan, throwing everything up from last night.

"Locker room, now!" Coach Stone yells when my eyes meet his.

God, he reminds me of my father.

"Set him up an ice bath," he tells one of the trainers. "Get in the showers and clean yourself up," he tells me. "Then come and see me."

I nod, stripping my practice jersey off. God, the warm water feels so good on my skin. My eyes close and my head rests on the tile, allowing the water to pelt my back.

What did I do last night? I pushed her away because I was upset and angry. That's what I did. I haven't had the guts to call and apologize to her yet. I miss her so much.

"Enough, my office," Coach Stone says from behind me and walks away.

I turn off the water and grab a towel. I don't bother to dress since he ordered me an ice bath.

"Sit," he says, pointing to the chair across from his desk when he spots me in his doorway.

I do as instructed.

"I warned you about this exact thing at the beginning of the season. I told you this needed to be a year with no distractions. When you and Ellery started dating, I thought it was going to be a problem, but then you started playing better than before. And then today you show up so hungover you can't throw a decent pass." He shakes his head, and I feel that disappointment deep in my bones.

"I'm sorry, but it's over. She's no longer a distraction."

He shakes his head and laughs. "She's more of a distraction than when you were dating her. You think the whole world doesn't know how you feel about her?"

"Why would they? I'm fine, Coach. It's better this way anyway. She's moving, taking a job in New York."

He rocks back in his chair and studies me for a long time. "Sometimes I think I should have gotten my psych degree. Actually, you have one, right?"

I nod, remembering my first class with Ellery when I had to tutor her.

"So, enlighten me, Rice. You and the girl you've loved forever get into a relationship. And now that you've broken up, she's not going to be a distraction?"

"Because I'm only going to concentrate on football." I cross my arms, trying to convince myself that this is the best thing that could've happened.

"Doubtful, but if you show up like this to another practice, I'm benching you for the next game."

"I won't. I promise."

This is my job, and I can't jeopardize it. I can't let the rest of my team down.

"Deal with this shit in the off-season. We're almost there, Rice. The third championship is within your grasp." He smiles.

He's right. If Ellery can put her career ahead of us, there's no reason why I shouldn't do exactly the same.

CHAPTER 29

ELLERY

A MONTH LATER...

I walk into the patient's room and sanitize my hands. Although it's not my direct patient, Amber, one of my attendings, asked for a second opinion.

The room is packed with people, and they're all wearing the New York football team's jersey, all their eyes on the television.

Since the Grizzlies are here playing for the division title against New York, I went out to eat with Bryce and Adeline last night. It's still weird not going to the games, but I will say that no one here has referred to me as Cooper Rice's girlfriend since I started here.

"Hi, I'm Dr. Wallace."

The room erupts in a roar. They all hoot and holler because the Giants got a first down. I look up at the television just as it shows Cooper on the sidelines.

I'm not one to bring trauma to myself, so I haven't watched a game since he broke up with me. Or when he said we needed a break and he left his apartment. We haven't spoken since then. I've wanted to reach out so many times, but I'm not sure what there is to say without causing each other more pain.

Cooper looks good. His face is stone-serious, his eye on the prize of winning the division, which will only propel Chicago closer to the chance to win the championship. I hate the fact that I wonder if he's hooked up with anyone else since me. If those pouty pink lips have been on another woman's. I shake my head and tell myself to stop thinking of that, it does no good.

New York is nothing like Chicago. I miss my smaller city where I knew every inch of my concrete world. My mom just moved here last week, so at least I'll have her to do some things with since I'm still trying to make friends.

Although the staff here is nice, I haven't really connected with any of them. Then again, my mind is constantly in another world, especially if I'm not working.

I still can't figure out why Cooper would think I wasn't one hundred percent in it with him. Bryce told me last night that it's just the way I'm wired, and when I asked her what she meant by that, she just said that my career has always been my priority.

"So, Mrs. Jennings, you came in complaining about—"

Another set of cheers sounds through the room, and everyone only gives me half of their attention. I grab the remote and turn off the television. They all grumble and stare at me.

"I'm sorry, but if you want to watch the game, you'll have to go into the waiting room," I say to what appears to be their two younger sons and daughter.

"Sorry, we're all just diehard New York fans. Excuse us for being so rude," the husband says, sounding genuine.

"I know it's a big game, so after I leave, feel free to turn it back on." I turn to the wife in the hospital bed. "Mrs. Jennings, you came in struggling to breathe, and I read in your chart that you've had a bad cough?"

The husband nods. "She's had this cold for a few weeks, and today she didn't seem like herself. We thought we'd come here for some antibiotics, but when they took her oxygen, they said it was low and brought her back here."

"I'm feeling better," she says, giving me a thumbs-up, but the woman has oxygen tubes in her nose.

I slide through a small opening and scan my ID to enter the computer. "Let's see if any labs have come in. You had a chest x-ray, right?"

It feels great to be interacting with a patient again, treating them.

I see that she has pneumonia, but they're going to have her do a CT scan due to her low oxygen level. I swivel in my chair. "Well, you have pneumonia, so we'll prescribe some antibiotics for that. But we're going to send you for a CT of your lungs just to make sure we're not looking at anything more serious. It's a precaution only, but we want to be sure. Just stay put for now, and hopefully we can get you out of here soon." I pat her shoulder.

"Thanks, Doctor," she says.

"You're welcome, Mrs. Jennings." I grab the remote and turn on the television. "Now, enjoy, but just keep it down a little."

They all cheer, and I shut the door to the room when I leave.

Before I make it over to the desk, I hear my name behind me. "Dr. Wallace, right?" Mr. Jennings says in a thick New York accent I'm still getting used to. I nod. "I don't want it to seem as if we don't care. That woman in that bed is my life, she's the beating heart at the center of our lives and our family is nothing without her. Should we get out of there so you can treat her?"

I smile softly. "It's quite okay, Mr. Jennings. I think she's just let this cold go on so long that it's now turned into pneumonia. I'll keep you informed."

"Thanks."

"You're welcome. Now go in there before you miss part of the game." He takes a step away, but then turns back around. "You're her, right?"

I frown. "I'm sorry?"

"My kids say you're Cooper Rice's girlfriend… or were?" This is the first time anyone has said something to me about Cooper since I arrived.

"I was, yes."

He takes my hand and squeezes it, startling me. "Hard to date someone like that, but I imagine it's hard to date someone who saves people's lives, too." He chuckles. "He's having the game of his life, you know."

"I saw that from my brief look at the screen."

He studies me for a beat. "Well, I do hope you find the kinda love like me and the Mrs. have, because to live without love, well, that's a wasted life. Everyone needs someone to come home to, someone who's in the trenches with you, someone who finds your kid just as entertaining as you. I'm sure you have a lot of work to do. Sorry." He waves his hand in front of himself.

"It's okay. Thank you for sharing."

"Maybe I'm just an old fool who wants everyone to be as happy as me." He winks and walks back to the room, and I watch him go.

One of his sons comes out just as he steps inside. "Bathroom?" he asks me.

I point to where he can go.

"Sorry if my dad talked your ear off. He's a sharer." He laughs and heads in the direction I pointed.

Pushing away what Mr. Jennings said, I input the orders, informing Amber that we'll get a CT scan done just to make sure there's nothing else going on, but the chest x-ray clearly showed signs of pneumonia. I ask her to come and get me when the results of the CT scan arrive, then go to my office.

In the quiet of my office, I pull up the game on my phone just to check the score, or so I tell myself. Chicago is winning, and just as I pull it up, Cooper jogs onto the field. It's early in the game, only the second quarter, so there's a lot of game left.

Someone knocks on my door, and my mind moves faster than my hands, causing me to fumble the phone while trying to turn it off. I look up once I stuff it in my pocket.

"Just checking on how your day is going." My dad's there in his white coat with his fancy new title stitched into it. He still can't stop coming down to the ER, and I wonder if he visits all the departments as much as he visits mine.

"Good. I actually got to interact with a patient today."

He chuckles. "Unfortunately, that is a by-product of the job once you climb the ladder. There's a lot of other things you have to handle besides dealing with patients."

He's not lying. It didn't take me long to realize that I went into this naively. I knew a lot of my time would be dealing with administrative and bureaucratic stuff, I just didn't realize how far removed I would be from true patient care.

"How's Cooper doing today?" he asks with a smirk because he caught me. Since he's the one who wanted us to break up, I'm not sure why he's even asking.

"They're winning." I offer the least amount of information I can.

"Guess your breakup hasn't affected his play."

I stare blankly at my dad. "It appears not. No."

"I wish I could say the same for you." He steps further into my office but doesn't sit down.

His comment feels like a slap in the face. "Am I doing a bad job?" I thought I caught on fast.

"You're doing a great job." He smiles. "I'm really proud of you. I get compliments all the time about you."

I frown. "Then what do you mean?"

He sets his hands on his hips and sighs. "You're not happy here, are you?"

"I am." I give him my best smile, even if I know it's fake.

"Ellery. I know I wasn't around a lot when you were younger, but I still do know you, and you're going through the motions here, but you're not happy."

Do I even open this line of conversation with my dad? I've never felt a sense of trust I think kids should feel telling their parents their hopes and dreams. I have never felt like I could be really honest. "I miss caring for the patients."

He nods, breaking the distance and sitting in the chair in front of my desk. "It takes some getting used to. Maybe you'll grow into it."

"Yeah, I'm sure I will."

"It's funny. I always used to feel like your mom got you the first eighteen years of your life and I'd get you for the rest. I thought we were replicas of one another. But your mother has been pushing her advice on me lately and made me realize that maybe you never wanted to be a doctor in the first place."

I shake my head. "No, I'm happy being a doctor, but…" I take a deep breath. This shouldn't be such a big deal to say, to admit to my dad as well as myself, but it is. It's years of engrained thinking I'm pushing up against. "I think I want more."

"This is more." He looks around the office with my name on the door.

"Not like that. I want to be the one caring for patients. I want to be the one who follows their cases through and sees the outcome, build a relationship with them."

He leans back and studies me for a second. "With all due respect, Ellery, you can barely handle it when you lose a patient in the ER. Can you really imagine having a closer relationship with them?"

"I've considered that." I've had a month to think about it

as I lay holed up in my apartment because my life, at least everything I knew of my life, is back in Chicago. I miss Cooper and Bryce. Hell, I even miss Damon. But I miss Cooper the most. The more I think about what he said, the more I wonder why I put all those stipulations on us. Why would I want to go slow when I had waited so long to cross that line?

"I guess you're more like your mom than me after all," he says, surprisingly not sounding mad. "Are you considering going back for family medicine?"

I nod.

"I knew you weren't happy here, but I thought that had to do more with Cooper than the actual job." I open my mouth, but he puts his hand up. "I want to apologize. I think I thought if I brought you here, you'd be able to really excel without the complication of Cooper. I should have never suggested the two of you break up." He shakes his head.

I look across the desk at him like I've never seen this man before. "Does mom have you in therapy or something?" I'm honestly asking because he's never talked to me like this.

I've always been afraid to open up to my dad, fearing this judgment. I didn't see him a lot when I was young, and when I did, he always praised me when I did well in school or showed interest in becoming a doctor like him. I think I thought that by pursuing the career he wanted for me, I was earning his love and respect.

He chuckles. "Your mom is none too pleased with me for moving us here. We've had some heated arguments, some involving you and how I treat you. She's a very persuasive woman."

"Dr. Wallace," Amber is in the doorway, sees my father in the chair, and backtracks. "I'm sorry. When you're available, I just wanted to go over Mrs. Jennings's results."

"No need. I was just leaving." My dad stands. "What do

you say? I'll cover for you so you can head over to the stadium?"

I shake my head. "Thanks, but I blew that chance."

"Oh, I think you could murder that boy's dog and he'd still want you." He leans in close, lowering his voice. "If you love him, go."

I squeeze his hand. "Thanks, Dad."

"Just let me know." He walks out of my office, and I step out to join Amber on the walk down the hallway to Mrs. Jennings's room.

"Everything looks good. There is a spot on her lungs that they want to keep an eye on, but other than that, it's just pneumonia." Amber smiles.

"Oh, that's good, but let's admit her overnight. Get some antibiotics in her and make sure her oxygen levels go up."

"I'll find her a bed."

"Do you mind if I tell the family?"

"Not at all. I'm a Buffalo fan." She heads over to the phones and computer while I knock on Mrs. Jennings's door.

I open it slightly and peek my head in. "Hi everyone."

"Oh, come in," one of the sons says.

Mrs. Jennings is sleeping, and they have the television on mute now. I glance to see it's already in the fourth quarter and only two minutes left on the block.

"Is it really tied?" I ask.

They all stare and nod. Oh, come on, Cooper.

"Well, I have good news, it's just pneumonia. There is a spot on her lungs that they don't think is anything but would like to keep an eye on it, so she'll have to go for another scan in a couple of months, but follow up with your primary care provider for that. We're going to admit her overnight to get the antibiotics in her system and make sure she's off the oxygen before leaving."

They all hug one another, clearly relieved.

"Thank goodness," Mr. Jennings says. He comes to me

and wraps me in a hug. "Thank you. I was scared for a moment when she'd become disoriented."

"That was from the lack of oxygen."

"I can't thank you enough." A tear drops down his cheek.

"Oh, Dad," the kids say in unison, sounding mortified.

He stares down at his wife with so much love that my throat squeezes shut. Not because I've never been looked at like that, but because I have, and I threw it away because I was scared.

Oh my god. What have I done?

Mr. Jennings smiles over at me. "It's never too late."

I shake my head. This man can really read people. "For us it is."

"I don't believe it. Go get him." He nudges me with his elbow.

"I…"

I don't really have an excuse. I'm the reason we couldn't make this work. My own fear stopped me from giving him all of me. The real question is, can I give him all of me?

"You have no excuse. If you love him, go to him, and when there are problems, love him harder. If you both truly love one another, you'll figure it out. I promise."

Why won't my feet move?

I think of how it felt to be loved by Cooper and know that I can't give that up. No matter how scared I am that things—mainly my emotions—aren't in my control.

"Shit, I think I'm going to. Oh my god! I'm going."

"Way to go!" The Jennings all silently cheer since the mom is sleeping.

I rush out of the room and call my dad to take over for me.

Please. Please answer.

CHAPTER 30

COOPER

The clock runs out, and the team on the sidelines rushes the field.

The Chicago Grizzlies are the division champs once more and on our way to the big game, crossing our fingers for the big game.

I head over and shake hands with Trent Yoders, the quarterback for New York, as well as a few other team members I know. We're shuffled out quickly, and I'm pulled aside to give an interview immediately.

"Congratulations," the interviewer, Samson, I think, says.

"Thanks." Someone tosses me a T-shirt and puts a hat on my head that says we're the champs in our division this year.

"You played one helluva game. How does it feel getting this much closer?"

I nod, knowing where he's going, even if he doesn't say it. "Good."

"That's it?"

"I'm not gonna celebrate until we're there. And then there will be the pressure to win. So, you'll see me excited when we're holding the trophy in our hands."

I don't tell him that the big reason why is that I recently

did that in my personal life. I thought Elle and I were golden and that we were endgame, only to figure out I was alone in that belief. She wasn't ready to get into a relationship with me. At least the same kind of one I wanted.

"And here comes the big guy himself, Coach Stone."

I hug Coach, and he pats me on the back. I slide out of the interview and head into the locker room.

The champagne sprays everywhere, thanks to Damon. I sip from the bottle but put it down, just wanting to get in the fucking shower and on the plane home.

It's been hard being so close to Ellery for the past twenty-four hours and denying myself seeing her. I almost caved last night after everyone went to bed. It would've been easy to sneak out of the hotel. But my willpower has won—I just don't know how much longer it will hold out.

All my teammates celebrate, and I stand by the locker, stripping off my jersey and pads.

"Way to go, Rice!" a woman's voice rings out, stopping all the chaos in here like the screech of a record.

I turn to find Bryce and Adeline in the locker room.

"Hey, babe, as happy as I am to see you, there are things here you shouldn't see." Damon approaches Adeline, covering her eyes.

"Damon, I'm a grown woman," she argues, but he doesn't remove his hand.

My vision shoots to Bryce, who only has her eyes on one thing: me. She shoves me, and I rock back in surprise.

"What the hell?" I glare at her.

"Stop being a baby. Go over to that hospital and grovel and get our girl back."

I shake my head and blow out a breath, giving her a look like she's crazy.

"You mope around all the time unless you're on the field. I gave you a full month and until this game to figure your shit out. And even then, only because Miles told me to, but this is your do-or-die moment. If you don't go to her now, I guarantee you're going to lose her forever." She pokes me in the chest.

"Jesus, control her, Cavanaugh." I look over at my teammate.

"No, because I agree with her."

"So do I." Adeline raises her hand around where Damon is covering her eyes. "Damon, I'm not Clover." She tugs on his arm.

"You're not going to see other guys' junk," he says.

"Damon's afraid ours are bigger," one of our teammates says to Adeline.

"Hell, get the fucking rulers out. I know where I stand in this group, but my wife isn't going to see it."

"This is ridiculous," Adeline says, and if I could see her eyes right now, I bet they'd be rolling. "Cooper, please listen to Bryce. We were with her last night. She misses you the same as you miss her. You think we can't see it, that you hide it, but it's there. The win today isn't as sweet, is it?"

Damn Adeline.

"There's no way it is. She's always been the first person you look for after a win. And I should know, I've been sitting next to her for years during your games." Bryce keeps coming at me. Every step I take back from her, she takes two toward me.

"Jesus." I lean in close. "She doesn't want me," I say through gritted teeth.

She looks behind me, hopefully cluing in that I don't want this entire locker room in my business. I'm their fucking captain, the leader on that field, and I don't want them thinking I'm some lovesick puppy dog.

Searching the area, she grabs my arm and tugs me into a room off the hallway. Miles, Damon, and Adeline follow, Adeline being led by Damon. Once we're behind a closed door, Adeline pulls away from him.

"That was highly unnecessary," she tells Damon, and he gives her some kind of look, and they grow closer as if magnets can't keep them apart. "Congratulations," she coos at him.

"Why won't you people leave me alone?" I ask, sitting in a chair.

"Because we love you," Bryce says, sitting down across from me. Miles is right next to her.

Adeline and Damon are in their private world in the corner.

"She doesn't want me, not the way I want her."

"And how is that?" Bryce crosses her arms.

"I don't want conditions on how I love her. If I want to see her, if I want to surprise her, I don't want to think about whether it's my night to see her or not. We just had different ideas of what it would mean when we got together, I guess. Hell, I'd marry her tomorrow and start a family the next day."

"And you don't understand why someone might get scared of moving so fast, especially when they waited so long to be with you?" Bryce asks, concern marking her features.

"If she loved me like I love her, she'd want those things too." I lean back in my seat, completely aware that might be ridiculous.

"Okay, I'm going to make this simple. We've both known Ellery for a long time. And what does she need in her life to feel safe and secure?" Bryce asks me like you would a four-year-old.

"Control," I say and roll my eyes.

"And to feel like she has that control, what did she become?"

"I know all this, but it's me, B, me." I jab my chest with my finger.

"Just answer," she says.

"A perfectionist."

"So, is she going to let you guys finally embark on a relationship only for it to capsize a month later?"

"Isn't that what happened?" Damon asks from the back of the room.

"Stay out of this," Bryce says without turning to look at him. "All those rules and stipulations were her needing to control what was happening between the two of you, but what she doesn't understand yet is that love is uncontrollable."

"So, tell her that." I cross my arms. I sound like a petulant teenager.

"I'm not the one who loves her despite her faults. Make her see it, Coop. Let her feel safe in your bubble, and eventually she'll loosen them up."

"You love her, right?" Miles asks.

"The first time I laid eyes on her, something inside me told me she was mine." I push a hand through my sweaty hair.

"Then why are you letting all this bullshit stop you guys from being together?" Miles asks. "So what if she lives here and you're in Chicago? You both have enough money to fly back and forth. Once the season is over, you can spend months here in New York with her. And let's be honest, you don't have decades of your career left." Miles smiles at Bryce like "aren't you proud of me," and she might give him a treat.

"I'm not even sure if she'd want me anymore," I say. That's what's stopped me from reaching out. The idea that she'll tell me it really is over—forever.

"Did you get to have all this success in football with self-doubt? Go get what you want, and if she says no, fight harder!" Bryce shouts.

I contemplate what they're saying. Will I ever be satisfied unless I know what we could have been if we'd tried? No. I don't know that I could ever move past it. I'd always wonder.

Bryce is right about Ellery—she does value control. In the

long run, does it matter that she's not ready for everything I am right now, as long as she is eventually?

Bryce is right, this last month has been horrible.

"I'm going," I say, standing.

They all cheer as I rush out of the room.

I don't stop until Damon calls my name. I turn around and have a T-shirt thrown in my face. "Don't get arrested before you get there."

Pulling the T-shirt over my head, I race out of the complex and into the first taxi that I find. I go to grab my phone, but I don't have it. Shit.

The taxi driver looks at me for a second, and I fear he's a lifer New York fan and might not drive me to the hospital, but he speeds off.

"What a game, huh?" He starts to make chit-chat.

"Sure was."

"New York should've taken you that year. To make that trade and give it to Chicago." He pounds on his horn.

I'm not going to say anything, but Chicago was where I was meant to be. I've never been as happy as when Elle tackled me to the ground because it ended up that we'd be in the same city. All the moments of my life with her run through my mind on the drive to the hospital.

My bruised ego got me where we are today. Never again. She should be with me, celebrating.

He carries on, and I let him act like an analyst who has studied the game for years. But my mind is too preoccupied to think of anything but Elle and if she's going to accept me back, but Bryce is right, I'm not taking no for an answer.

What feels like a lifetime later, the taxi pulls up to the curb, and I open the door and freeze. "Shit. I have no money." I turn back to him. "Sit tight, and I'll figure out how to get you some."

"Don't worry about it. Go get your girl."

How the fuck did he know?

"Thanks?" I get out and slam the door. My cleats almost make me fall on my back when I hit the concrete, but I recover.

Walking as fast as I can into the emergency room, I go to the nurse's desk. "I need to see Dr. Ellery Wallace."

She looks at me, her mouth hanging open. "Oh my god, you're…"

"Yep, I know who I am. Can you please get her?"

The girl who looks so young she must be new continues to stare, and someone walks past and scans a badge to get back into the ER, so I slide through the door, causing her to snap out of her trance.

"Elle!" I yell. "Ellery!" I walk down the hallway, looking into every room.

"What the hell?" Dr. Wallace, and not the one I'm looking for, comes out of a room, standing in front of me with his arms crossed. "You can't just come in here and interrupt our operation."

"I'm sorry, sir. Where is Elle? I need to talk to her."

He studies me for a second. This is a wall I hadn't intended to face. The man doesn't want me with his daughter, and I'll have to plead our case to him, but the only fight I have in me right now is the one for Elle—she matters most.

"Please tell me where she is."

"Coop?" That's her voice, I can't be imagining it. I turn and find her standing with her coat on and a bag slung over her arm.

"Ellery!" I run over, slipping on my cleats and ending up on my knees right in front of her. Oh well, I need to grovel anyway. "God, you look beautiful. I've missed you so much."

"What are you doing here?" she asks.

"I'm here for you."

She says nothing, so I continue. I take her hand in mine.

"I'm here to tell you I was wrong. We can make this work. I'll do whatever it takes. I'll get us each a membership in one of those private plane groups so we can go in and out of small airports and save time. I'll set you up with a driver to meet you on both ends of any flight, and I'll hire you an assistant to clean your place and do your groceries, so you don't have to worry about that stuff if you're visiting me. We can figure this out. And after the big game, I'm all yours. I'll move out here and explore this city just like we did eight years ago in Chicago. But I need you in my life, Ellery, and not as a friend. You know, just to be clear. If you're not ready for the other stuff, that's fine. But I can't live without you."

"Cooper..." She places her hand on my cheek.

I squeeze my eyes shut. "Please tell me I'm not too late to fix this, Elle. Please."

"You're not too late," she says in a soft voice. "Except I'm coming back to Chicago. Not right away, I have some responsibilities here, but I'm moving back. I want to go into family medicine."

My heart is beating so hard I can hear it in my ears, and I have to check that she's saying what I think she's saying. "And us?"

"Yes, to all of it. I'm sorry I didn't see it all when you did, but I do now. I was scared. What if we ruined it by going too fast? What if it affected my career? And I don't know what kind of mom or wife I'll be, and that scares me. But I do want those things. I'd rather screw up with you than be with anyone else and not have those things."

"You're going to be an amazing mom. But we don't have to worry about that right now. Just come home with me where you've belonged since junior year."

She gets down on her knees, too. "This time, we're sealing it with a kiss." She wraps her arm around my neck and pulls me into her, her lips smashing into mine. When things get a little heated, Dr. Wallace clears his throat.

"Are you off?" I ask, staring at her purse and coat.

"I was coming to get you." She looks over my shoulder,

and I turn to see a gentleman in a New York jersey smiling over at us.

I smile wide. "You were?"

"Yeah," she says, and I'm clearly missing something, but I don't care. "Let's get you showered."

"As in, both of us are going to shower me?"

"Rice…" Dr. Wallace warns.

"Sorry," I say, standing, then helping Ellery up and wrapping my arm around my girl's shoulders. I'll never let her go again.

Once we're outside, the taxi driver is still there, so we climb in.

"Why did you come to get me?" she asks on our way back to the stadium.

"Because you've always been my girl, and you always will be."

She grabs my shirt and tugs me closer. "Good line, Rice."

"It's the truth."

"Ditto."

EPILOGUE
COOPER

The clock runs out on the game, and the confetti sprinkles from the sky. In seconds, I get bombarded by every player on our team.

We did it. Three championship wins in a row. I'm a shoo-in for the Hall of Fame after I retire, whenever that will be.

I'm being interviewed by Samson again, and his typical stern impression shifts to a smile right before someone jumps on my back. I don't have to see her to know who she is because the feel of her, the smell of her—everything about her—I committed to memory years ago.

"Congratulations, babe! I'm so proud of you." She kisses me on the cheek.

"I must say you're much happier this time than at the division championship," Samson says.

Ellery is moving back to Chicago this week. Things between us are different this time around. She's not holding herself back, and I'm not pushing us forward. I waited ten years for her to be mine, and she is. That's all I really want. She's moving in with me, but sadly we're leaving The Den. Along with Miles and Bryce.

Ever since Rowan Landry moved in, there have been more

than enough parties. And that's what The Den was meant for, honestly. When I bought the building, I pictured bachelors there enjoying everything it and the area had to offer. But it doesn't suit any of our lifestyles anymore.

She slips off my back and into my arms. God, her body up against mine, there's no better feeling. "Let's go get your award," she whispers, assuming I'll win the MVP, but we had a lot of great players today, including Bradley.

"I'm not sure it's mine," I whisper back, taking her lips and kissing her until I hear the clearing of a throat.

I look around to see Bradley standing at our side. I guess Samson moved on since he's interviewing Miles now.

Bradley puts out his hand in front of me. There are rumors he wants a trade. Feels he's too much in Damon's shadow and wants to go to a team where he shines. I understand, we only have a set number of years to make our mark in this profession. You never know when an injury can take you out.

"I just wanted to say, thanks. I know we've had our problems, but you're a great quarterback and captain." I shake his hand, his words meaning more to me than anyone else's.

"I selfishly hope you end up with us, but if not, good luck. Any team would be better for having you."

We shake, and he nods his head. "Ellery."

"Bradley." She smiles.

"Let's go, man." Damon smacks me on the back, Clover in his arms, and Adeline right next to them. Last year was his year, and I hope this year is mine.

We all end up huddled at the end of the platform they wheel out. Orange and blue confetti still streams down to the ground.

Our GM gets handed the trophy and passes it to Coach Stone, who signals for me to come up. I kiss Ellery on the cheek and join him.

"We'd never be here without this man. He is consistent and steadfast and never gets detoured." Coach eyes me, and I smile because I did a little this year, but I recalibrated and tried not to let my personal life affect my performance. "Three Super Bowl wins in a row puts us all in elite territory. We'll take it." He raises the trophy in the air and hands it to me.

I step up to the microphone. "I'm not alone on that field, every one of these guys worked their butts off to reach this goal. Not to mention our fans. Chicago, another one comes home to us!" The stadium roars to life.

I pass the trophy down to Damon, and then he passes it to Miles. Each player takes a picture with it.

"And now for the MVP," the announcer says, getting handed the award.

I don't have to win MVP to know I played a great game. Tons of players deserve it, and I don't care because I have the one thing I've always wanted. I look at Ellery, and my eyes lock with hers as they make the announcement.

"No surprise here, Cooper Rice!"

Ellery screams, and even I'm surprised. She rushes over and I pull her to me, kissing her and taking her hand to drag her back over to the microphone with me.

"Thank you!" I raise the award in the air. "But every player on the field and coach on the sidelines was an MVP today. This is for all of us." I hold it up, and everyone cheers.

I hug Coach and everyone else, about to pull Ellery from the stage, but when I turn around, she's still standing there, asking for the microphone.

What is she doing? I look at our friends, and they all shrug. Well, the boys do.

"Sorry, just one more thing," she says into the microphone.

I think people are confused and don't know how to react because it gets oddly quiet.

"I've known Cooper for a long time, and I selfishly put him in the friend zone because I never wanted to lose him. See, what not everyone knows about Cooper Rice is that he's a good guy, he's faithful, and he genuinely has your best interests at heart. He'd run a mile in a snowstorm to save me. I didn't want to give that up for what could be some fling we'd get out of our system. As many of you are aware, we tried and failed once this year, and that's on me. But I never dreamed I could live this life with you, Cooper. Every day I'm happier than the last, so…"

She digs into the pocket of her coat, falling to one knee and opening a box with a silver band inside. "Marry me?"

"Elle…" I can't think of anything else to say—I'm in shock.

"I was a fool, Coop. I want to be your wife and have your babies and grow old with you. What do you say?"

I rush back over to her, ready to pick her up when she shoves the microphone into my mouth. "Yes," I say with a laugh.

She stands, and I pick her up and swing her around. "You're still getting the best proposal ever, you know that, right?"

"I can propose to you, it's not the 1950s." She takes the ring out and holds it for me, sliding it on my finger. "It looks good on you."

"Not half as good as your diamond ring is gonna look on you."

The stadium goes wild, and I take my new fiancée down the stairs to take her to the nearest jewelry store.

One Month Later…

All six of us—well, seven, including Clover—stand outside The Den.

Bryce rubs her small belly, and Miles kisses the top of her

head. Adeline clings to Clover, and Damon's arms are around them both. This place holds so many memories for us.

Even Ruby has decided to leave, shutting down Peeper's Alley. Said she didn't understand the young customers anymore and wanted to take it easy.

A moving van pulls up, and then another one behind it.

Rowan opens up the gates after coming down from his apartment and stares at all of us. "You all look like you're about to cry. You can visit anytime you want."

"No, they can't," all the women say in unison, probably thinking of what will happen here now that three bachelors are back to living in the apartments.

Tweetie comes out of one of the moving trucks. His personality is bigger than Damon's, and I wonder if he'll ever settle down. There was a time I didn't think Damon would.

"Who died?" he asks.

"Their single lives." Rowan laughs.

Tweetie walks over to the gate and pulls down the sign that reads *The Den* and smacks on another sign. He smirks over his shoulder and follows Rowan through the gates. "Go live your happily ever afters." He shoos us with his hand. "We'll take over from here."

The gate shuts, and we all laugh because Tweetie's sign reads *The Nest*.

It's official, we've been replaced by the Chicago Falcons, and I think I can speak for all of us when I say that we couldn't be happier.

BONUS EPILOGUE

FIVE YEARS LATER

I rock our new baby boy, Luke, in my arms while his big sister, Alexa, is sitting next to me quietly after being bribed with a bag of candy. Keeping this crew quiet for Cooper's retirement speech is harder than when the waiting room for my family practice is filled with crying toddlers. Cooper was blessed to play another five years in the league and was the last of the three guys from The Den to retire.

I look to the stage where Ronnie Michaels is in front of the microphone. "This man needs no introduction. He comes from quarterback stock. His father played for the league as well, but it was him who led his team to three consecutive championship games, earning the MVP in his final big game. He's one of the lucky ones who got to spend his entire career with the Chicago Grizzlies. He'll be greatly missed, but he should be proud that he made his mark." Ronnie holds up the plaque he's presenting to my husband.

Cooper stands from his chair behind Ronnie, dressed in the three-piece suit we took him to buy a month ago. After all the alterations, it fits him perfectly, showing off his broad shoulders and muscular legs. Our eyes catch and he smiles down on us from the podium. I demanded he not make me cry with his speech, but I have a feeling he's going to break his promise.

"Thanks, Ronnie," he says, shaking the GM's hand. Ronnie nods and sits down giving Cooper the stage.

He's quiet for a moment, staring down at the plaque in his hand, taking it in. I see him swallow hard, emotion getting the better of him and the wife in me wants to give Luke to Adeline and save him, but his head lifts and he looks out at the audience. "What can I say? I feel like I was just sitting in the draft room, waiting for my name to be called. I can't believe I'm at the end of my career, but there's a new stage of my life I'm excited to experience. Thank you, Chicago. Thank you to the Grizzlies family. You've always made me feel welcome and at home during my time here. I couldn't have asked to play for a better team in a better city. I'm not sure who was looking out for me on draft day, but damn I owe them big."

The room roars with applause. He looks at me and I shake my head.

He chuckles into the microphone. "I promised my wife I wouldn't make her cry."

The room laughs, and Adeline and Bryce both glance in my direction.

"Ellery, you are the one person who has been by my side through all the ups and downs during my career. The bad games, the good games, the amazing games. You've seen me at my worst, at my best, and definitely at my happiest. You've blessed me with two awesome kids. Marrying you was a dream come true. I loved you long before being able to call you my wife. And now I get to spend the rest of my years with you."

Tears are at the cusp of my eyelids, but Luke fusses and I

have to give him my attention. I rock him a little and give him his pacifier, but he's having none of it.

Alexa drops her candy and little candy-coated chocolates sprinkle all over the floor. "MOMMY!" she shouts. Face heated, I quickly bend down to pick them up while Luke wails in my arms.

"Hold on a second." Cooper rushes down and squats to help me pick up the chocolates.

"What are you doing? Go back up there," I whisper.

"I've got this guys." Adeline falls to her knees beside me with Clover right next to her.

"I'll help. Come on Alexa," Clover says with her hand out.

I shoot them a grateful look.

Cooper takes Luke from my arms and walks back up to the podium. "Sorry guys, when duty calls you gotta answer. I no longer have the excuse that I'm studying the play book or watching tape."

The audience laughs.

Luke quiets in his dad's arms, staring up at his father like I often find myself doing—like he's an enigma. The man handles it all with the grace and patience of a saint.

"Thank you again. No matter where I go, Chicago will always be home." He lifts the plaque, kisses it, and raises it in his hand.

The crowd claps, everyone standing, including me.

"And who knows, maybe in twenty years or so you'll have another Rice on that field." He looks to Luke and smiles.

Cooper walks off the stage and hands Luke to Damon, coming over to wrap his arms around me. "Not one tear, huh? Cold."

I smile. "More like your kids started acting out as if I paid them to save me."

"It couldn't have been more perfect timing."

"I've trained them well." I laugh. "Congratulations, you're officially retired."

"And now you're really stuck with me." He grins.

I take his head in my hands. "Good thing I love you so much."

He looks at me for a beat, his expression intense before he speaks again. "You're my everything, Elle. All of this means nothing without you. Thank you for supporting me all these years. For sitting in the first row every home game, for telling me when I'm in my head. For massaging my arm and shoulders after rough games. And most of all, thank you for giving me my future." He slides out of my hands and takes Luke back, handing him to me. Then bends to pick up Alexa in his arms.

"Daddy, candy?" she says.

"In a second."

"You are all my life. I can't wait to live out the next phase of my life with you, watching our kids grow until I get you all to myself again."

A tear falls down one cheek and then another one.

Cooper laughs.

"Damn you," I whisper.

"Why is mommy crying?" Alexa asks her dad.

"Because she loves me," he says.

"I love you too, but I don't cry." She frowns.

He wraps his arm around my back and pulls us all in for a big family hug. "My entire world in a two-foot radius." He kisses my temple before we're bombarded by everyone who wants to congratulate him.

As I watch him make his way through the room, shaking hands and hugging, a small pit forms in my stomach. Without football, it's just me, just us, what if he thinks we're enough, but we're really not?

"Stop it," Bryce sits down next to me.

"What?"

"Overthinking. Adeline and I have both been there already. You guys will find a new rhythm, new roles. He'll probably get bored and get some hobby or maybe start a second career." Bryce's hand lands on my thigh.

"The first season was the hardest," Adeline says from my other side. "Damon would watch a game and go off about what they should be doing on the field, second guess his retirement... but their bodies aren't built to last forever in the league. He did say how nice it was not to be downing Ibuprofen and having ice baths the next day after a game." She chuckles.

"It's an adjustment but if we can get through it, so can you." Bryce smiles down at Luke. "Since we're all in Chicago they can form some retired football players daddy group. Take the kids to preschool and go for walks in the park."

We all laugh together.

"Is it weird that all our husbands are all retired and we still work?" I ask.

Adeline took a break from working but now she's back to teaching after Damon retired.

"Oh, I couldn't spend the entire day with Damon," Adeline says. "I love him but..."

"Yeah, I'm with you." I smile at her.

The boys walk over, Cooper babyless while Damon holds Hannah, their one-year-old and Miles has Jackson, their two year old.

"We should go celebrate," Miles says.

"Where are we going to go with seven kids?" Damon sits next to Adeline. While she fixes a bottle for Hannah, he tries to soothe her with the pacifier.

Miles and Bryce had twins who are turning five this year. Landon and Christian both resemble their dad. When they tried again, hoping for a girl, they got Jackson who looks like his mother.

Damon and Adeline's second daughter looks just like her older sister, a perfect combination of both their parents. I'm not sure if either of the other couples are done having kids yet. Cooper and I haven't made that decision either, although the late nights with Luke are taking a toll on us.

"I forgot to tell you all, I scored tickets for the Falcon's game next weekend," Cooper says.

Cooper still owns The Den which is now called The Nest. The Falcons have taken it over, so they always give him tickets to a suite when there is one available.

"And I'm off, so you all better be there," I point at the rest of the group.

We chat for a while longer and after we say our goodbyes, return to our newly renovated house in Chicago. It's close to the train, so I can get to my clinic easily. Neither one of us was ready to move to the burbs just yet.

Both kids are asleep and Cooper is sitting up in bed with no shirt, watching ESPN. As I come out of our bathroom, putting lotion on my arms, I unapologetically stare at him. He is so gorgeous, so manly, and so, so mine. I can't believe this man decided to spend the rest of his life with me.

"Are you going to come join me or just gawk?" he says without turning in my direction.

"I figured you'd be tired after your day. It had to be emotionally draining." I break the distance pulling the covers back and sliding in under them.

He wastes no time in swinging his arm around my waist and tugging me so I'm half under him. "I'm never too tired for you."

"Are you sure you're not upset? Wish you had another year?"

He chuckles and nuzzles his head into my neck. "We both know, my arm wouldn't allow it. And I want to be able to pick up my kids. In the last thirteen years, my body has been beaten to hell. I'm more than ready."

"Okay."

He gets on top of me, his knees pushing my legs open. I wrap my arms around his neck and bring him down to kiss me. The minute our lips connect, the pace increases since it's not every day we can have sex anymore. We start stripping one another as if we only have five minutes before a buzzer will go off and say try again next time.

"My first mission is to get you on a vacation, just you and me."

"And who is going to watch the kids?" I ask, then moan as he takes my nipple into his mouth. "Your mom and dad would love to."

"Not sure what we'd be coming back to."

He lifts his head. "They'll be fine and just think, we'll be able to have sex for longer than five minutes," he says, his hand sliding into my silk shorts.

Sure enough, ten minutes later, we're both catching our breath on our backs. Yeah, as good as this is, I miss having the time to explore each other's bodies, tease one another. "Just give me the dates and I'll turn in my vacation."

He laughs. "That's my girl."

The following weekend, we're all in the box at the Falcon's arena, watching Chicago's professional hockey team play against their rivals, the Houston Hornets. We all opted for an adult night only, getting sitters for the kids.

The skating has always impressed me, how fast they move down the ice while maneuvering a small black disc with a stick.

"You're not going to leave me for a hockey player, are you?" Cooper wraps his arms around me, resting his chin on the top of my head.

"No, but some of these guys have impressive skills."

"Which number is Rowan again?" I ask.

"There, number ninety-four." He points, and Rowan scores just as I find his number on the jersey.

The crowd goes crazy and the Jumbotron shifts to a woman in the stands who is clapping. I'm guessing that's his girlfriend or maybe his wife? Before I can see if the number on her jersey is the same as Rowan's, the camera shifts to some young boys sitting beside an exhausted-looking mom. Yeah, I know how she feels.

"I hope you get more tickets. I enjoy watching all the action," I say.

"Keep talking about how impressive they are and I'm never going to bring you again," Cooper says.

"How about you take me home and you can show me how impressive your skills are?"

He inhales a deep breath and groans. Taking my hand, he pulls me toward the door. "Sorry guys, we have to go," he calls out.

We ignore all the complaints from our two best friends and head home where Cooper proves yet again, that his skills still reign supreme.

Can The Nest live up to the reputation
The Den had?
Find out in our newest hockey romance series following the
Chicago Falcons!

COCKAMAMIE UNICORN RAMBLINGS

Oh, the friends-to-lovers trope! It's our evil stepsister, our Achilles heel. We know our readers love it, and we do enjoy writing a couple with history, especially when one person secretly loves the other, but for some reason, it's our kryptonite.

Since we decided on this trope early on in the prequel On the Defense, we'd painted ourselves into a corner and had to find our way out. There were a lot of ways this story was going to go in our preplanning. Most of which, we barely remember now. With the friends-to-lovers trope there are only so many reasons a couple wouldn't have crossed that line yet that make the story plausible.

We don't like other women or men drama in our books. Piper doesn't like love triangles at all (she finds them too stressful and they give her anxiety), but we had to bring Bradley in because we needed his presence in Ellery's life to spur Cooper into action. And who doesn't love a jealous hero?!? Of course, the gang knew they needed to be together, so the cabin scene was planned and one of our favorite scenes in the book.

In the end, we think we did their story right. Although they had feelings for one another, they spent all those years as just friends to make sure they'd remain in each other's lives, hence they they had to find out what it would be like if they didn't have one another. In the end, they each jumped into each other's arms and toward their happily ever after!

As always, we have a lot of people to thank for getting this book into your hands!

Nina and the entire Valentine PR team.
Cassie from Joy Editing for line edits.
Ellie from My Brother's Editor for line edits.
Rachel from My Brother's Editor for proofreading.
Hang Le for the cover and branding for the entire series.
All the bloggers who read, review, share and/or promote us.
The Piper Rayne Unicorns in our Facebook group who always think we score a touchdown! LOL

Every reader who took the time to read this book! Thank you for granting us your most precious resource—time. We don't take that lightly and appreciate it more than you'll ever know!

Now that The Den has been renamed The Nest by one of your favorite guys, Tweetie, what could be next? Hockey! We're heading back onto the ice! We hope that you join us as we leave the football world for a bit and head back to the world of professional hockey. Rowan Landry's story is next! Yes, we're still making you wait for Tweeties story—but it's coming!

xo,
Piper & Rayne

P. S. For those of you who don't know Tweetie, we suggest heading to the Hockey Hotties series and checking it out. That said, you don't need to have read any of those stories before digging into the Chicago Falcons stories. We just think you'll enjoy them!

ABOUT PIPER & RAYNE

Piper Rayne is a USA Today Bestselling Author duo who write "heartwarming humor with a side of sizzle" about families, whether that be blood or found. They both have e-readers full of one-clickable books, they're married to husbands who drive them to drink, and they're both chauffeurs to their kids. Most of all, they love hot heroes and quirky heroines who make them laugh, and they hope you do, too!

ALSO BY PIPER RAYNE

Chicago Grizzlies

On the Defense

Something like Hate

Something like Lust

Something like Love

Lake Starlight

The Problem with Second Chances

The Issue with Bad Boy Roommates

The Trouble with Runaway Brides

The Drawback of Single Dads

The Baileys

Lessons from a One-Night Stand

Advice from a Jilted Bride

Birth of a Baby Daddy

Operation Bailey Wedding (Novella)

Falling for My Brother's Best Friend

Demise of a Self-Centered Playboy

Confessions of a Naughty Nanny

Operation Bailey Babies (Novella)

Secrets of the World's Worst Matchmaker

Winning My Best Friend's Girl

Rules for Dating your Ex

Operation Bailey Birthday (Novella)

The Greene Family

My Twist of Fortune

My Beautiful Neighbor

My Almost Ex

My Vegas Groom

A Greene Family Summer Bash

My Sister's Flirty Friend

My Unexpected Surprise

My Famous Frenemy

A Greene Family Vacation

My Scorned Best Friend

My Fake Fiancé

My Brother's Forbidden Friend

A Greene Family Christmas

The Modern Love World

Charmed by the Bartender

Hooked by the Boxer

Mad about the Banker

The Single Dads Club

Real Deal

Dirty Talker

Sexy Beast

Hollywood Hearts

Mister Mom

Animal Attraction

Domestic Bliss

Bedroom Games

Cold as Ice

On Thin Ice
Break the Ice
Box Set

Charity Case
Manic Monday
Afternoon Delight
Happy Hour

Blue Collar Brothers
Flirting with Fire
Crushing on the Cop
Engaged to the EMT

White Collar Brothers
Sexy Filthy Boss
Dirty Flirty Enemy
Wild Steamy Hook-up

The Rooftop Crew
My Bestie's Ex
A Royal Mistake
The Rival Roomies
Our Star-Crossed Kiss
The Do-Over
A Co-Workers Crush

Hockey Hotties
Countdown to a Kiss
My Lucky #13
The Trouble with #9
Faking it with #41

Sneaking around with #34

Second Shot with #76

Offside with #55

Kingsmen Football Stars

False Start

You Had Your Chance, Lee Burrows

You Can't Kiss the Nanny, Brady Banks

Over My Brother's Dead Body, Chase Andrews

Plain Daisy Ranch

The One I Left Behind

The One I Stood Beside

The One I Didn't See Coming

Standalones

Single and Ready to Jingle

Claus and Effect

Made in United States
Orlando, FL
28 January 2025